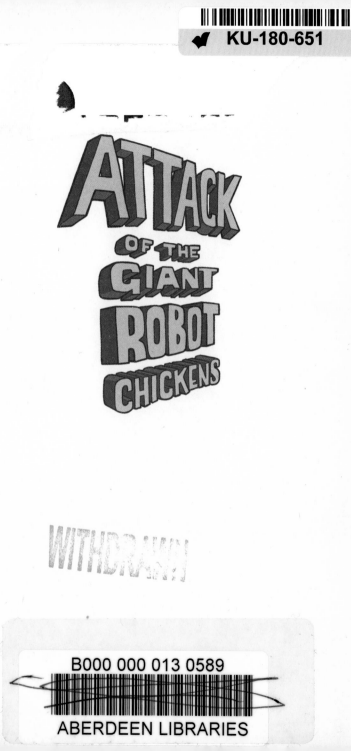

ATTACK
OF THE
GIANT
ROBOT
CHICKENS

ATTACK OF THE GIANT ROBOT CHICKENS

ALEX MᶜCALL

 Kelpies

Kelpies is an imprint of Floris Books
First published in 2014 by Floris Books
Second printing 2014

The publisher acknowledges subsidy from
Creative Scotland towards the publication
of this volume

 This book is also available
as an eBook

British Library CIP data available
ISBN 978-178250-008-7
Printed in Poland

To my friends and family, for helping with reading, supporting me and forgiving me the incessant puns. And to you, the reader. Because you're reading my first book and that's just so cool.

CHAPTER 1

My big brother's hobby was the end of the world.

I don't know why, but he was fascinated by it. He'd talk about it all the time, all the different ways that civilisation as we knew it could come crumbling down. I had to listen to his plans to escape from tsunamis, meteors, floods, aliens and his favourite, zombies. He would never shut up about zombies. The walls of his room were covered with maps, and he'd drawn all sorts of lines and arrows on them. He was ready for anything.

I never got it. I mean, he was a normal sixteen year old the rest of the time. He hung out with his friends, he got good marks at school. He even had a girlfriend, though I think she was as confused about his hobby as I was. I mean, he wasn't even that geeky. Why would he have such a weird obsession?

I asked him about it once. He just shrugged.

"I like to be prepared," he'd said.

"For what?" I asked. "Zombies? Aliens? That's never going to happen."

He'd laughed at that. I can still see him, standing above me, the light shining off his glasses and his blond hair. "I guess you're right."

"So why do you do it?"

He'd sat down to tie up the laces on his boot, bringing himself down to my level. "I guess I just like the way it makes me feel. Safe. Like I'm prepared for anything, you know?"

I thought about that for a moment. "That's kind of weird," I told him.

He'd laughed again. He was always laughing. He never took anything really seriously. "Yeah. But everyone's a bit weird." He'd stood up again, kicking his feet a few times to make sure that his shoes stayed on. "Come on, little brother. Time to go to the movies."

Then he'd ruffled my hair and we'd left.

That had been eight months ago. I hadn't seen him since.

I shook myself out of my memories and looked around. Sam and Mike were standing above me, on the stairs that led to the upper floor of the Central Library. They were slouched against the wall, trying to show how unbothered they were by everything, but I could see how tense they were. So I decided to lighten the atmosphere with a joke.

"Hey guys, have you heard this one before?"

They both turned and looked at me, not impressed. I wasn't surprised. No one around here had a sense of humour.

"So there was this library, a bit like this one, only with a librarian. And one day a chicken walked in."

"Shut up, Jesse," Sam said. He was the leader on this expedition because he was the oldest. He was also a lot taller than me, though just about everyone was. That didn't mean I had to listen to what he had to say.

"So the chicken walks up to the counter and says to the librarian, 'Book, book.'"

Sam tried to ignore me and said to Mike, "Why do you think they haven't turned up yet?"

"Dunno," said Mike. I'm not sure why Sam bothered asking. 'Dunno' was one of the only things that Mike ever said. Rumour was that it was his first word.

"So the librarian gave the chicken a book and it walked out the door. The next day it came back and the same thing happened. It walked up to the librarian and said, 'Book, book.' The librarian gave it another book and it walked out the door."

Sam continued to talk over me. "I mean, we've got the food they were asking for. They should be here."

I didn't give up. "This kept happening day after day and eventually the librarian begins to wonder where all his books are going. So the next day, as usual, the chicken comes in, goes up to the counter and says, 'Book, book.' The librarian gives it a book and it turns around and walks out of the door. But this time the librarian follows the chicken."

Sam gritted his teeth. "Seriously, Jesse. Shut up."

"He follows the bird and it goes out of the library

and down the road. Then it goes down a farm track, still clutching the book under one wing. It reaches the farm and struts over to a pond. In the middle of the pond is a frog and scattered around it are all the books that the chicken has been taking out of the library. The chicken goes up to the frog and puts its present on a lily pad, going, 'Book, book.' And the frog takes one look at it, shakes his head and says, 'Reddit, reddit.'"

I beamed up at the other two. They failed to burst into laughter. They didn't even chuckle. They just glared at me. I swear the end of the world does something awful to people's sense of humour.

I took a quick look around, then got to my feet. The sunlight had moved up the wall since we had come in. "We'd better go now, guys."

Sam looked at me in disgust. "They aren't here yet. We'll wait until they turn up."

I shook my head. "They aren't coming. Trust me."

"Why should I?"

"Because I've been sent out more times than you two put together." It was true. I reckoned our leader had something against me. "The Library gang rely on the food too much to miss it. If they're hiding then that means that a Catcher's in the area."

That got their attention. It didn't matter how tough any kid pretended to be, none of us wanted to be caught. "Are you sure?" Sam asked.

"Try this," I said, and put a hand flat on the stairs. The other two glanced at each other and copied me.

After a moment I could feel a faint tremor shake the building. By the looks on their faces they'd felt it too.

"We have to get out of here," Sam hissed. "Come on, Mike. Jesse, grab the food."

The two older boys pushed past me. I looked at the white plastic bag sitting on the stairs, then followed them.

The Aberdeen outside wasn't in ruins, like you'd expect a city to be after the world had ended. The granite buildings had managed to endure for centuries. Eight months without being looked after hadn't had much effect. The grass in the small island across the street had grown long and leaves were everywhere, but that was the only notable difference. That and the silence. This used to be a busy part of the city but now there was no one. It was like the set of a TV show, waiting for the actors.

If I was lucky I'd be able to get away before the drama started.

Sam and Mike had already run to the left and I walked after them, going slower, taking my time. The ground shook again, more noticeably. It was getting closer.

By the side of the theatre there was a stone staircase that curled between the buildings on either side and led down to a street. I walked briskly towards it, not pausing to look around. If I hesitated for even a second I might be seen and captured. And on the stairs I would be safe. It couldn't follow me down there.

I kept thinking about my brother as I walked. It was something I'd found myself doing every time I was in danger. Sometimes I could almost feel him there with me, keeping me safe like he always had. I could imagine him here where I was, doing much better than me. Always prepared.

But he hadn't been prepared for this. Then again, who could prepare for the uprising? Who could have expected it?

I made it to the stairs and my heart rate decreased slightly. I took a deep breath and began walking down. The stairs were old worn stone and still slippery from the rain of the night before. I walked carefully, not wanting to risk a fall. The thing following me wouldn't be able to get me, but there were others who could.

I don't know what things were like elsewhere but in Aberdeen we quickly fell. Mankind didn't have much of a chance. After all, we were outnumbered six to one.

The ground shook again just as I reached the bottom of the stairs. I looked back, shrinking close to the ground and then freezing, trying not to be seen. There was a shadow, then the bulk of the thing itself strutted across the passageway behind me, blocking out the light. Just a large indistinct shape.

Mike and Sam were waiting for me at the bottom. I felt touched for a moment, before realising that they couldn't have gone any further without risking being seen. I sighed.

"This way, guys."

I led them round the back of His Majesty's theatre, climbing a fence and crawling through some overgrown bushes as I did. Then I motioned them to stop and slowly leaned around the corner of the building.

And there it was, crossing the bridge, heading towards the Art Gallery and the centre of town as if having a leisurely weekend stroll. One of the things that had been hunting us for two thirds of a year.

A giant mechanical chicken.

I just stared at it for a moment, then shook my head. Nope. My brother had never seen this coming at all.

CHAPTER 2

Living in a chicken apocalypse is not quite what you'd expect. It wasn't as if everyone just woke up one day with a chicken standing on their chest, staring into their eyes. Even looking back there were no obvious signs that it was coming, like mysterious disappearances or random large eggs discovered. It had begun as a normal day. I'd gone into town with my brother to catch a movie, but he'd left me at the cinema in Union Square while he went to find some of his friends. He couldn't just call them because his mobile had stopped working.

I guess that was the first sign.

The second was probably the giant robotic chicken that crashed through the roof.

I can't really remember the rest of what happened that day. I started running, people screaming all around me, desperate to find some place to hide. I managed to survive by falling in with some guys hiding out in the train station. I didn't know who they were, and they didn't know who I was. We were all too scared to care.

A few months on and I think they had stopped being scared and just regretted letting me hang around.

I thought about this while crouched behind the library. After we were sure that the chicken was gone we hurried back to the train station. By this point Sam had noticed that I'd left the food bag behind.

"You idiot," he growled at me, still not confident enough to raise his voice. "I gave you one job and you left it behind. What are we going to tell the boss?"

"He'll understand. Those people need that food and this way they'll owe us one."

He gave me a little shove and I stumbled. "Yeah, because we don't need food at all. What was I thinking?"

I moved out of the way of another shove and glared at him. "We've got enough to last us for a while. They don't. And at least this way someone gets use of it. If we'd been captured then no one would have had the food."

By this point we had entered the train station. I stepped further away from Sam and looked around. Even after months of living here, I was still impressed by the sight.

Aberdeen train station had been built back when Britain still had an empire and liked to show off by making things big and shiny. The glass roof was high above us and still mostly intact, letting in the weak spring sunlight. The marble floor shone, though there was litter scattered everywhere. The air was colder in here and I huddled deeper into my jacket. Security points were positioned between the benches and the tracks, but as we were already on the rails they didn't serve much point. We were used to clambering through them by now.

Sam and Mike ignored me as we made our way to one of the trains that was still waiting for passengers who would never come. We'd been lucky; a sleeper service to London had been idling on the tracks when the first attack came. It was warmer than most of the other trains and we all got beds. Compared to how some others lived it was almost civilised.

To get there we had to get up off the tracks. As I scrambled up the makeshift steps that we'd made out of suitcases, I saw a silhouette in the door of one of the carriages and Boss Noah stepped forward.

Like the apocalypse surrounding us, the leader of our little group wasn't what you'd expect. He was skinny, with glasses and a serious expression. Like the rest of us his hair was beginning to get a bit long and stood out from his head like a ginger halo. His T-shirt was a plain brown and unlike some he hadn't taken the excuse to dress in the latest fashions scavenged from shops. He was also one of the oldest here, at fourteen, but that wasn't what made him the leader. If it had been zombies instead of chickens then I don't think he would have survived very long, but against the chickens he was level-headed and never took any chances. He seemed to be fitted for the not-so-glamorous roles of organisation and motivation. He couldn't have fought his way out of a wet paper bag but that wasn't what was needed here. His intelligence could be the saving of us all.

I don't think that he liked me either but at least he was good enough not to show it. Except by sending me out on all those expeditions.

He stepped lightly on to the platform as we came towards him.

"Sam, Mike," he said. Then his gaze swerved to me. "Jesse. Where's the food?"

Sam immediately puffed out his chest and stepped forward. "There was a Catcher patrolling," he said. "We had to get out. I told Jesse to grab the food, but he left it behind at the library."

Noah sighed and gestured. "Come inside and tell me about it."

So we did, sitting on bunks in Noah's bedroom. Because he was the boss he got a room to himself. As this was perhaps the only perk of the job we were OK with him having it. Sam told the story by himself, with Mike nodding occasionally beside him. When they finished, Noah fixed me with his piercing look. "Is all this true?"

"Yup," I replied, grinning at him. "I'd call the mission a success."

"A success?" Sam spluttered. "But we didn't get any of the clothes we were going to trade the food for."

I shot him a look. "We've got more clothes than we're ever going to need. We've got all of Union Square and there were plenty of clothes shops in there. It was never about the clothes. It was about gaining another group's trust. And by leaving the food we've done that."

Noah nodded, though he didn't look happy about agreeing with me. "Jesse is right. We need to keep reaching out to other groups if we're going to survive. The Library Gang might not have anything to offer us right now but we could probably use them in the future."

Sam was even less pleased. "He disobeyed a direct order and left behind vital supplies and you're just going to let him get away with it?"

"Just leave it, Sam. What's done is done. Now go get something to eat."

Sam pushed past me and stormed off, Mike trailing behind him. I waited a bit then followed, but Noah called me back.

"Jesse, stay close, would you? I've got a job for you later."

I felt a flutter of apprehension but just nodded. "I'll be in the dining car," I told him.

To get to the dining car I had to pass by the Radio Room. Somehow the chickens had managed to take down a lot of the electronic communications and most of our mobile phones had run out of charge in the months since the first attack. But we had managed to salvage some stuff.

I looked into the room in passing and nodded to the kid on duty. He ignored me and continued messing around with the radio, turning the dials and getting nothing but static. We had a couple of smart phones and a laptop as well but we only used one thing a day. The ones we weren't using were hooked up to a solar charger outside. It was the only way we could get any information on what was happening – and even then there was a lot we didn't know. We didn't even have any idea what the chickens were. I mean, they could have been anything from aliens to mutants that were somehow advanced enough to build these machines.

We didn't get much news but we got a bit, mostly from America. The UK government had fallen pretty quickly and the chickens had spread into Europe, where they were slowly pushing forward. A lot of world leaders had made various speeches, but the attack had caught everyone by surprise and they were pretty slow to do much else except for talk. There was fighting going on but nobody was anywhere near overcoming the chickens. Canada and Australia were supposed to be getting ready to launch a counter attack but that hadn't happened yet.

There was nothing new to hear so I left the room and continued towards the dining car. The walls were papered with pictures, warning people about what the chickens could do. Surprisingly, I was one of the few people who had actually seen a robot chicken. A lot of people who'd seen a Catcher had been taken. Noah had told us to draw posters so that everyone knew what we were dealing with. Some of them were pretty good. There was a stylish shot of a chicken with lasers coming out of its eyes, one showing the explosive eggs they laid. There was even a diagram of the inside of a giant robot chicken. It had a kid being pecked up and swallowed, sliding down the chicken's throat and being trapped in its stomach. A lot of people had got freaked out by that one. As I slid the door to the dining car open I was just curious how the artist had known what it was like.

Maybe with a zombie apocalypse we would have seen some action... a lot of blood, maybe. But with the chickens we were in danger, but not able to actually go anywhere. Our free time was usually spent in the dining car of the train, talking, playing cards or reading. I found myself a seat and started doodling in a notebook I'd found in Union Square. With half an ear I listened to those around me.

The conversation was always the same, different people going through the same motions. It would be about TV shows or YouTube videos from when there *was* TV and YouTube. Games that they'd played on the Xbox or PlayStation. Causal stuff, like you'd hear in any playground.

And sometimes, when someone had had a bad day or the monotony was getting hard to handle, they'd talk about their families. Where they were, if they were still free. Everyone had given up hope that any parents were still free – the Catchers took the adults first – but there were older and younger brothers and sisters that no one knew about.

I could hear a couple of girls talking about it.

"I mean, my sister was smart," one of them was saying. "She was in the Guides and everything. I'm sure she's OK."

I wasn't sure. Guides were tough, but being tough hadn't helped the army.

"And we don't know the chickens attacked everywhere in Scotland. They could just have hit the cities. Maybe if we got far enough away we'd be safe. We should try it some time. Get as much food as we can and just follow the train lines south."

No one who went outside the city ever came back. I mean, it might be that they got to safety. Or they could have just been captured. I know which one I thought was more likely.

The other girl was smarter than her friend.

"Look," she said, putting an arm round her friend's shoulders. "If there was help out there then they'd come and get us. No adult in Aberdeen managed to hide for more than a few days. We're safe here. It wouldn't be smart to leave."

I was just nodding to myself when the first girl burst into tears.

"I miss my sister so much. Where is she? Where could she have gone?"

And that was the worst thing. No matter what we told ourselves, whether we thought our family and friends were captured or whether we hoped they had escaped somewhere, we just didn't know. We had lots of thoughts, lots of guesses – but in the end they were worth nothing.

The girl's sobbing was beginning to get to me, reminding me of my brother and how much I missed him. I closed my notebook and got up, ready to leave. If Noah wanted me, he could find me in my room.

I'd just reached the door when it slid open and the Boss himself was standing there. He smiled at me then noticed the girl wailing. A frown creased his brow and he gently pulled me through the door.

"Do you know what's up with her?" he asked, sliding the door shut on the noise.

"She misses her family."

He ran a hand through his hair. "We all miss our families. Think she'll be OK?"

I shrugged. "For a while."

He nodded. There wasn't really much else that could be said.

"What do you think of that group up at the library?"

I frowned at him. Was I about to be told off?

"I don't know. Like we said, I never saw them. They must be reasonably organised, to have survived this long. They knew there was a Catcher in the area before us as well; they'd cleared out. Though I guess they could just have a good view. Do you agree with Sam? You think I shouldn't have left the supplies?"

He shook his head. "Look Jesse, whatever Sam said, you made the right call. You do know that, right?"

I sighed but nodded. "Yeah, I know."

Then he fixed me with that special look of his that let me know trouble was coming. "I'm glad you got back. I've got a special job for you."

I grinned at him, though my heart had started fluttering a bit. I ran through everything that it could be in my head, but nothing I could think of was that bad. "Oh?"

He nodded. "The Ambassador's back."

"Huh," was all I could think to say, as the bottom dropped out of my stomach.

This was going to be terrible.

CHAPTER 3

When the end had come most people had survived by grouping together, like the Train Station Gang. The chickens had targeted the adults first and foremost and ignored everyone under the age of sixteen. A lot of us didn't know how to look after ourselves, so it was either club together or get grabbed.

The Ambassador wasn't like that. I wasn't sure what her real name was, but she survived by herself. She travelled around, finding each of the groups and trying to befriend them. I think she gave Noah the idea of trying to make friends with the guys at the library. She probably knew more about Aberdeen as it was now than anyone else.

She was also a little scary. And she was yet another person who didn't like me. So whatever involved her probably wasn't that good for me.

Noah took me along the train to where she sat, passing back through the dining carriage on the way. It was quiet again, full of kids just talking and reading. None of them looked up as I passed.

The Ambassador was in a compartment at the end. Like almost everyone else in the world she was taller than me and built quite solidly. Not that she was fat (no one was fat any more), but there was no question that she had muscles. At thirteen, she was a year older than me and a year younger than Noah. Her hair had been long to begin with, and was now bound back in an impressively large ponytail.

She stood up from the bed and glared at us as we came in. Or maybe it was just at me. I returned the glare with a measured stare.

"So what's this about?" I asked.

She looked at Noah and this time she was definitely glaring.

"Him?" she said. She clearly wasn't impressed.

Noah shrugged. "Is there a problem?"

"The joke-teller. You're sending him."

I don't like people talking like I'm not there, so I chose this moment to butt in. "Sending me where?"

"Noah, you know how important this could be," the Ambassador said, ignoring me. "I was expecting you to come with me yourself, or at least send someone important. Why him?"

"Why him what?" I asked. The Ambassador shot me a look but didn't answer. I felt the need to get a response from her.

"All right. How long do chickens work?" She still didn't reply, so I finished the joke for her. "All around the cluck."

She stared at me for a moment longer, then looked back at Noah. "You see?" she said.

Noah scratched the back of his neck and kicked me gently on the leg. "Jesse, stop being an idiot. This is important."

"All right. I'll cluck up."

He shook his head and started leaving. "He's the one you're getting. Have fun." Then he slid the door shut behind him and was gone.

The Ambassador looked at me levelly for a moment, then sighed. She sat back down and gestured that I should as well, so I perched on the bed across from her.

"So what's the job?" I asked.

She shrugged, then said, "I think I might have a way to take down the chickens."

I stared at her for a second then swallowed.

"You're joking."

"I believe joking's your thing," she replied.

"All right, I'll bite. How?"

She looked annoyed for a moment. "I don't know."

I smirked. "OK, so you have a way to take down the chickens, but you don't know what it is?"

She took a deep breath and seemed to count to ten in her head. "I've run across this guy who might know. He's been living in Aberdeen University and when I last talked to him he said that he was close to discovering something."

I thought about it for a second. It might be possible.

And if the guy was telling the truth then this could be huge. "Where do I come in?"

For the first time she looked angry, not just annoyed. "This guy's a bit of a jerk. Even worse than you. He won't tell me what it is because he reckons I don't belong to any group. He wants a representative of one of the bigger groups in the city to guarantee his demands will be met."

"His demands?"

"Yeah. He wants food and clothing. And a few other things I think."

I nodded. There were tonnes of clothes and enough food that we didn't have to worry for a while. Luckily there weren't that many of us.

"Well that shouldn't be too hard. Should I load up some stuff now?"

"He wants it on a regular basis."

That was more of a problem. A one-off gift of food? Not really an issue. Giving it to him weekly, or even monthly, would be much harder. And that wasn't counting having to carry it across the city to him if he was set on staying at the university. That would be incredibly dangerous.

"Does Noah know about this?"

She stood up, towering over me. "Of course he knows. And he agrees with me. If the information turns out to be good then he's willing to take the risk."

"Of course he is." I got up as well. Having the Ambassador looming over me was unsettling. "So when do we set off?"

She gestured towards the door. "Right now, of course. Get your stuff. We're leaving."

All that I had left in the world was a backpack that I kept stowed under my bed. I can't say that anything in it was exactly mine. It was filled with stuff I'd nicked from the various shops around, especially the nearby camping shop. It had been put together in case I ever got chucked out of the gang or they came under attack and I had to run. This seemed pretty close to getting chucked out, so I heaved it up on to my back and joined the Ambassador on the platform.

She saw me and raised an eyebrow. I could see that she'd got a similar bag on her back.

"Great minds," I said to her. She huffed, obviously insulted, and walked away without saying anything.

"So are we bringing this guy any food or anything?" I asked, hurrying to catch up with her. I couldn't see any extra supplies on her, though she might have had some in her backpack. She shook her head.

"No, just seeing you will be enough."

"Yeah, right. When are things ever this easy? How will he know that you didn't just grab some random kid?"

The slight hesitation before she took her next step told me that she hadn't thought of that, but she quickly recovered. "That would be a problem no matter who I brought. This guy is smart, though. He'll see sense."

She didn't say anything else, just led the way over the turnstiles and out to the front of the train station, where there was a huge empty foyer. The place gave me the creeps, especially when I was the only one there. Maybe it was the size, and feeling so alone where there should have been so many people. Maybe it was memories of the day the chickens came. I don't know, I'm not a psychologist. But I didn't really like being there.

Instead of taking us out of the front door, the Ambassador led us straight ahead to the bus depot. I followed, frowning.

"Which way are we going anyway?"

She didn't look around. "We're going to head along the quay then get up on to Union Street where it turns into King Street. Then we just follow it until we get to the university."

I stared at her for a moment. I didn't know the names of all the streets around here but I knew roughly what she meant. "We have to walk past the quay? That's kind of out in the open, isn't it? Why don't we just get on to Union Street right away and follow that?"

She shook her head, slowing just enough for me to walk alongside her. "Union Street isn't safe."

"Why?" I'd heard that before from Noah. I guess he'd heard it from the Ambassador, but I didn't know the reason.

"It just isn't. You wouldn't believe me if I told you."

I was pretty sure that I'd believe anything at this point, but I didn't press the issue. If she wasn't going to tell me then she wasn't going to tell me and nothing I said or did would change her mind.

By this point we were at the bus depot. The gates to the street were open so we headed towards them.

"So..." I began but she cut me off.

"Are you going to talk the entire way there? 'Cause that's going to get old really fast."

"You might find that you grow to like my conversation."

"I really doubt it. You never talk about anything sensible."

"You don't know me, so how do you know that?"

I wasn't really offended, but it was nice to talk about something, even if it was me.

She sniffed, cautiously making her way through the gates and out on to the road beyond. It was a dual carriageway, cluttered with cars jumbled together. Beyond the mess I could see a white metal fence. I'd been out here a few times and knew that it protected a clear strip of land and then the ships that still lay in the harbour. There was something pretty creepy about it. It was yet another place where I didn't like to go, though at least I wasn't alone. To my knowledge no one had tried getting on the ships.

We began moving carefully through the cars. We'd almost got to the traffic lights before she answered.

"I've heard enough about you to know. All you ever do is make jokes."

I shrugged. "Yeah, fair point. But there's a reason behind it."

"Oh, what? To annoy everyone?"

"Nope."

"Then why?"

I shook my head. "Oh, it doesn't work like that. You have to tell me stuff before I'll tell you anything."

"Why should I tell you anything?"

Her voice came out a bit loud and we both froze. I was pretty sure that we were safe this close to base. If there was anything around then they'd have been spotted by our lookouts a while ago. Noah had put them all around the station and Union Square. They could probably see us right now. But there was nothing that would get us caught faster than being careless.

After about five minutes we unfroze and started walking again, staying close to the buildings. If a chicken did come for us we might be able to get inside and hide.

"Because you know more about me than I know about you," I hissed to her. "You know who I am and probably where I come from. I don't know where you came from or why you don't hang around with groups like everyone else. I don't even know your name."

She didn't answer me, just kept on walking, not saying anything. I trudged along behind her. I felt a bit ashamed about my outburst, but why should I trust her when she obviously didn't trust me?

After a few minutes we came to a wide street with no cover whatsoever. I took a deep breath and dashed up it, only stopping when it had safely narrowed again. I turned back, expecting to see the Ambassador following me but she was just standing there, looking at me like I was an idiot.

"Come on," I called back to her.

"We're not going that way." She pointed along the road that we had been following, which led further along the quay. "We're going this way. We can't go on to Union Street."

I was beginning to really want to know what was on Union Street. Whatever it was really seemed to have her spooked. I tried to smile reassuringly at her.

"We'll only be on Union Street for a short while. Trust me in this."

Maybe something I said earlier had stuck because she took a deep breath then dashed over to where I was standing. The street wasn't that narrow. A giant chicken would have been able to fit in here. But it was still less dangerous than the quay had been.

"If we get caught I'll never forgive you," The Ambassador hissed at me. I rolled my eyes.

"Yes, your Ambassadorness."

The street wasn't that long but it seemed to take ages to walk up it. It was only when we were getting to the end that I realised that the Ambassador was dawdling. She really didn't want to go there.

From a purely tactical sense I agreed with her. Union Street was the main street in Aberdeen and that meant that it was wide. A whole army of giant chickens could march up it and we wouldn't be able to do anything to stop them. If we were spotted, we wouldn't stand a chance.

But King Street was almost as big. I didn't know my way around the city as well as she did but if the Ambassador had problems with Union Street because of its size then she could probably have found a better way. There was definitely something wrong here. If something could freak out the Ambassador that badly then it couldn't be anything good.

Finally we reached Union Street. I took a quick look around before darting back to the Ambassador.

"I can't see anything," I told her. It suddenly occurred to me that the chicken I'd seen earlier could be around here, but I decided that she didn't need to know that right now. She was getting panicky enough as it was. "We should make it."

She nodded, trying to hide her emotions behind a mask of confidence. I could respect that. "Then let's go."

We ran for the corner where Union Street turned into King Street. Whenever there was a chicken around I liked to move slowly. I didn't know much about chickens, but from what I remembered from a documentary they could only see movement. Or was that dinosaurs? Anyway, moving slowly and carefully seemed like a good idea. But when there weren't any around it was even better to move fast and get into cover, instead of being left out in the open.

I glanced down Union Street, just to see if I could see anything that could make the Ambassador that scared. I thought I caught a glimpse of something white in the distance but we were in cover before I could get a good look.

The Ambassador was gasping as if she'd just run a marathon, instead of the short distance. I decided that the white thing in the distance was yet another thing that she didn't need to know about. Instead I pulled a bottle of water out of my backpack and offered it to her. "Are you all right?" I asked.

She took a quick gulp from the bottle before straightening up and nodding. "Yes. Thanks, Jesse."

I think it might have been the first time she used my name.

"No problem, Ambassador."

She had started walking forward again but stopped, uncertain. Then she said. "You don't need to call me that. They just called me that because I move between the groups. My name is Rayna."

I smiled. Progress.

CHAPTER 4

We walked in silence. I didn't want to push the little trust that Rayna had given me and she seemed relieved by the quiet. Besides, it was usually a good idea not to make noise. You wouldn't think it but cities without people can be eerily quiet and any noise can echo. So I spent my time looking at the shops to either side of us and memorising them. The group was still pretty well stocked for supplies, but they would run out eventually and it was always good to know where else to go to look for them. The great thing about a chicken attack in the middle of the day was that most of the shops were still open, meaning that we didn't have to break in to any. I got really excited when we passed a Morrisons. There weren't all that many supermarkets near the centre of town and it could potentially keep us in food for the rest of the year.

After about forty minutes, we came to a crossroads and the four streets stretched out in every direction, long and straight. The one building off to the right was barely one story high and when I glanced left I found myself looking at a wide expanse of green grass and bushes. It looked too open. Open was not good. Open got you caught.

Rayna seemed to sense that I wasn't happy. "What's the matter?" she asked.

"It just seems a bit... exposed," I said weakly. "What's a field doing in the middle of Aberdeen?"

She looked at me strangely. "It's not a field. It's a metre wide space, then there's a lorry park or something."

"It's still pretty open."

She nodded. "I guess, but this is the fastest way there. Look, there's a pretty solid building along here that I sometimes camp in. We can rest up there for a while and get something to eat. Are you hungry?"

I was, but I hadn't wanted to mention it. Breakfast had been a long time ago, before I'd set off to the library, and it was midway through the afternoon by now. I followed Rayna as we walked carefully across the intersection and towards the building she had been talking about. It was pretty impressive, long and brick, with a turret on the wall at either end. I wasn't sure if you could get in them or not but a turret was a turret.

She let us in the back door and up some stairs to the second floor. She wasn't kidding about having camped there in the past. There was a sleeping bag, a table with a few chairs and a couple of boxes full of what looked like tins. Even more impressive was the gas-powered stove with the pots and pans. We had one back at base but we didn't use it that often. Getting the fuel for it wasn't easy. Mostly we just ate things cold. My stomach, which had been pretty quiet up until now, suddenly twisted in anticipation of a hot meal.

Rayna saw the look on my face and grinned. She carefully lit the stove and gestured at one of the boxes. "You can pick anything you like from there."

I went to have a look and found it full of tins of soup. I looked through for maybe half a minute before returning, clutching two tins in my hands. She glanced at the label before raising an eyebrow. "Chicken soup?" she said, her voice sarcastic.

I shrugged. "It seemed fitting."

She laughed a bit and emptied both tins into a pot, putting it onto the stove and pulling out a spoon to stir it with. "You're odd."

"Everyone is," I replied, echoing my brother. Then I swept my arms around in a circle. "The whole world is."

"True enough," she said. The soup quickly came to the boil and she pulled the pot off the stove. Then she handed me another spoon.

"No bowls, I'm afraid," she said. "We'll have to share the pot."

I wasn't bothered and had already taken my first spoonful of chicken before she'd finished talking. It was still very hot and I almost burned my mouth as I swallowed, sending it rolling down my throat in a warm, delicious wave. It had been so long since I'd had anything hot, let alone anything that was well cooked, that I had to remember to let Rayna have some as well. She was a lot daintier than me and took a lot longer. I had to stop to let her catch up.

"Hey, Rayna. Why did the chicken end up in the soup?"

She looked annoyed, then sighed irritably. "I don't know. Why did the chicken end up in the soup?"

"Because it ran out of cluck!" I beamed at her.

She stared at me a second then went back to eating. "Ha ha. Very good. Are you going to keep doing that? Telling jokes?"

"Oh. Probably."

"Could you not? Please?"

I was about to tell her no, but then I stopped and held up a hand.

"Feel that?" I asked.

She looked at me, exasperated. "If this is another joke..." she began but I cut her off.

"No, no, I'm serious. I think a Catcher is coming."

She immediately got out a glass and poured some water into it. Sure enough, it began trembling a second later. One of the giant chickens was nearby.

We both hit the floor. She got down before me because I grabbed the pot of soup and brought it with me. She looked at me weirdly, but we'd probably have to stay down for a while and I really needed that food.

Still, I could get to that later. First I had to find out what was going on. I crawled across to the window and took a look.

The Catcher was closer than I thought it would be, plodding its two-legged way along. It was so close that I could see the detail on it. Each of the feathers seemed to have been carved individually out of metal and they rattled slightly with each step. The beak looked realistic as well. This wasn't good. When they'd first attacked, the giant chickens had seemed pretty basic. Just a round body on a pair of legs. If more time was being taken to make artistic changes then that suggested that the makers weren't too concerned about being attacked. Whoever they were. Worse, it meant that there were more of them being made.

There was a rustling noise and Rayna pulled herself up next to me. We were both quiet for a second, watching as it came level with our building. It was zigzagging slightly, wandering about as if drunk, and it seemed to be peering into random windows. Silently, we both lowered ourselves out of sight.

"Hey, why did the chicken cross the road?" I asked, only half joking. My heart was racing. I actually really wanted to know.

"It's probably hunting for us. It must know that we're in the area and that's why it's acting oddly. I just can't figure out how it got wind of us so fast. We haven't done anything that could have alerted it."

I shrugged and pulled the pot closer to us. "It was

probably already in the area. I've already seen one today. Maybe they're increasing the amount of patrols that they're sending out."

She frowned, but she picked up a spoon as well and joined me in eating. "I hope not. We've been pretty lucky so far. There are still a lot of kids out there."

"I reckon the Catchers don't really care about us."

She looked at me, her head cocked slightly to one side. "Why do you say that?"

"Well, I've seen some of what those things can do. They can fire lasers from their eyes and their beaks can peck through rock. I think that if they were really serious about catching us we wouldn't have a hope. I think that they only catch us when they see us so that we keep our heads down and don't interfere."

She took another spoonful. "But they captured all the adults."

"Yeah, the ones who could attack them and do them harm. I think they just don't see us as the same sort of threat."

Most of the soup was gone by then and our spoons were scraping the pot edge, trying to get every scrap of food that we could. I gave up first, now feeling pleasantly full, and heaved myself up to look out of the window. The chicken seemed to be gone.

"You know, we can still be a threat," Rayna said. "Especially if this plan goes ahead."

I turned and watched as Rayna packed everything away and got ready to move again. "I hope you're right," I said. "Because if they're sending out more patrols, something's got them spooked."

We set off again after giving the chicken a ten minute head start. Ten minutes should be more than enough. Their legs were just so much longer than ours that they could cover the ground a lot quicker. We were right. Once we'd left the building there was no sign of it except for a few cars nudged into different positions. Still, I glanced at the sky, worried. It would be night soon and I didn't think we had enough time to get back to the train station.

Rayna led us up to College Bounds, which was a cobbled street that led straight to the university. I couldn't help but be impressed. She really knew her way around and had been able to take us the entire journey without missing a step. It was only once we were outside the university that she paused, uncertain.

Aberdeen University has been around for hundreds of years. The part we were standing outside, Elphinstone Hall, towered into the sky. It wasn't that big compared to, say, a skyscraper... but skyscrapers are modern things. This building was old before skyscrapers were even thought of. I had the feeling that it would be here long after we (and the chickens) were gone.

Eventually Rayna started walking towards the

entrance. I fell into step beside her. "Nervous?" I asked.

She shook her head. "I was just trying to work out where he'd be," she said. Aberdeen University was pretty big. It could take a while to find the guy she was looking for, especially if he didn't want to be found.

As it turned out, he did want to be found, if the large piece of paper with, 'In the library' written on it was any clue. It was taped to the inside of the door where it wouldn't be seen by giant chickens but would be seen by anyone coming through the entrance.

"Great," Rayna said through gritted teeth, grabbing the sign and yanking it off the door. She turned on her heel and stalked back the way she had come.

"What's wrong?" I asked, hurrying after her.

"I don't like the library building. It looks creepy."

I had to agree with her. The library looked like a bad modern architecture joke gone wrong. It was a giant cube, towering high above everything else around it. Where all the other buildings around here were made out of stone it was almost entirely glass. About halfway through construction it seemed that the designers had noticed how much it stuck out and tried to lessen the effect by camouflaging it with zebra stripes. All in all, it looked weird and out of place. And it didn't look like a great place to hide.

Once inside it was a little better. Seven floors curved away above our heads, each opening to the foyer we were standing in. There was a café off to our left and a round white donut in the middle of the floor was probably the admittance desk. There was no sign of anyone around.

"Hello? Glen?" Rayna called.

There was movement on the top floor and someone stuck his head over the bannister. It was too far away for me to see anything expect blackish hair hanging messily around a wide face. "Ambassador? Is that you?"

"Yes," Rayna called back. "I've brought a representative with me from one of the city gangs."

"And it's not...?"

"No, it's not Cody's. This guy's from the Train Station Gang."

"Excellent. Bring him up."

The head retreated from view and Rayna turned to me.

"Come on. We'll have to take the stairs; the lifts don't work."

"Who's Cody?" I asked, but Rayna didn't answer.

We clambered over one of the barriers and into the nearest stairwell. The stairs looked like something you'd find in a multi-storey car park, just solid slabs of undecorated concrete. It even smelled faintly like a multi-storey car park. And climbing seven flights of those stairs was not fun.

We emerged at the top, gently panting, to find the person we'd come to speak to sitting at a table surrounded by stacks of books. He'd somehow managed to stay quite plump, despite a shortage of food and the exercise he must have got by walking up those stairs every day. He looked up as we approached and smiled slightly. I might have been paranoid, but it didn't look like a nice smile. "You took your time," he said.

"Then why don't you use your genius to fix the lifts?" I shot back immediately. He looked surprised.

"Excuse me? Who are you?"

Rayna stepped between us. "He's the one you wanted me to bring, Glen. The one from a city gang, to assure you that we're good for the price. Because you didn't trust my word."

Her voice hardened slightly at the last bit and I took a step away from her. Glen didn't appear to notice.

"Yes, well, I've got certain needs. You're just one person. How was I to know if you could provide what you said you could? In fact how am I supposed to know now? This could be anyone that you dragged up from anywhere. Did you bring any food?"

Rayna looked at me, annoyed that I'd been proved right. I didn't gloat; I'd save that for later. Instead I dug around in a pocket of my jacket before pulling out a chocolate bar and tossing it to Glen. He looked at it in surprise and immediately ripped the wrapper off before stuffing it into his face. I watched him, feeling slightly jealous. I'd been looking forward to doing that.

Rayna waited until he'd finished, then continued talking. "Is that enough for you?"

Glen shook his head again. "Don't be silly. It helps me trust you, but one chocolate bar isn't anywhere near the price that I was asking for. You're going to have to do better than that."

I took a step forward, threateningly. I wasn't actually going to attack him but he didn't know that. Rayna grabbed my shoulder.

"So what do we have to get?"

Glen thought about it for a moment. "Well the first week's delivery would help. That way I know I could trust you."

I butted in before Rayna could answer. "We can't do that. You're asking for a fair amount of food. We can't just let you have it before we know if what you're offering's worth it."

He sneered at me. "So don't ask for my help. I'm giving you a chance to stop the chickens. I just need to know that I will be given what I ask for in return."

"If your information really does all that it's supposed to then you should just give it to us anyway. If we can defeat the chickens then you'll profit too."

He laughed. "What do I care? I'm happy enough where I am. I've got enough food to survive for a while and the chickens can't get me in my fortress here."

I laughed right back. "Your fortress? This place?" I gestured around at the glass walls of the library.

"Haven't you ever played Angry Birds?"

He scowled at me and Rayna chose this moment to butt back in.

"So, Glen – you need to know you can trust us first?"

He turned back to her. "No offence, Ambassador. I just need to know that your word is true."

She shrugged. "All right. So why don't you pick something else for us to get, something that's not quite such a big deal but that will still prove that we can be trusted?"

He thought about it for a second, then nodded.

"I've got it. I know exactly what you can get me. Wait here a moment."

He disappeared off among the shelves. Rayna and I just had time to exchange a confused look before he was back, flipping through what looked like a thick book. As he got closer I saw it was a catalogue.

"It was here somewhere..." Glen muttered to himself, then nodded. He turned the catalogue round and handed it to Rayna, tapping an item. "There. I want that."

She took the book and gave it a quick look. "A TV," she said. "You want me to get you a TV?"

"Not just any TV. That very specific TV."

"Why?"

He just smiled at her. "I need it. Now, are you going to get it for me or not?"

"I guess. It won't be easy, though. Which shop even stocks this?"

She turned the catalogue round to get a look at the front cover as Glen answered.

"Argos."

"Argos?" Rayna asked, fear creeping into her voice. I realised what the problem was.

"Yes, Argos," Glen replied, all grins. "You'll find it on Union Street."

CHAPTER 5

"Look, I'm sure that there's something else we could get him. A nice new jacket or something. You don't have to go if you don't want to."

Rayna grunted at me and kept walking. I tried again.

"You don't even need to go. I'm sure that he trusts you. I'm probably the one at fault. So why don't you stay with him and I'll go get it alone?"

She seemed to consider that for a while then shook her head. "No, we've got to do this. If we get split up then we might not be able to find each other again. And we can't just get something else. If we don't bring back exactly what he wants us to then he's not going to trust us and this whole thing is pointless. So we go, we get the TV, then we get out as fast as we can."

I sighed and nodded. "I guess you're right. But what has you so freaked out about Union Street?"

She stopped for a second as if considering telling me, then shook her head and walked on. "You still wouldn't believe me. Now come on."

I followed her, wondering if she was right. After

Glen had told us what he wanted, she'd nodded in a sort of trance then turned to leave. I'd followed her, sending a threatening glare back over my shoulder at Glen so he'd know not to double cross us. I'm not sure it had worked; he was taller than me as well.

After that we'd gone to a retail park just up the road and spent the night camping in the sofa store there. This morning, Rayna had seemed better, but she still wasn't in what I'd call a good mood. So as we walked I tried to take her mind off it.

"Hey, I've got a question," I said to her. She didn't look at me, just kept on walking.

"If it's a chicken joke then I'm going to punch you in the face," she said, matter-of-factly. Yikes.

"No, no, it's not that," I answered quickly. "I was just wondering... if Glen has enough food to live comfortably, why is he wanting more? Was he bluffing?"

She nodded. "Yeah, I think so. Certainly he's wanting a lot of food on a regular basis."

"How much?"

"About a hundred cans a week."

I whistled. "Seriously? That's a lot. What's he wanting with so much food? He already looks well-fed."

She shrugged. "I think he's covering for someone. Though he won't say it, I think that he's got a little group of his own in there. My guess is that only he is ever around because then if someone turns him in somehow only he'll get taken and the others will be safe."

"People do that? Turn other people in to the chickens?" I was horrified. I'd never heard of that happening before.

Rayna had been relaxing up until now, but she tensed up again. "Yup. It can happen."

That put a damper on that conversation and we walked along in silence for a while. Eventually I broke it.

"You know there's another explanation," I told her. She looked back over her shoulder and down at me.

"Yeah? What is it?"

"He could just be really greedy."

She looked at me for a second then burst into laughter. I joined in, pleased to have cheered her up.

"I mean look at him," I carried on. "He doesn't look like he's in any danger of starving to death."

She kept on laughing, though she managed to choke it down and change it into chuckles. I copied her. Laughter could be heard and though we hadn't seen any evidence of chickens so far, it didn't mean that there weren't any around.

"Why can't you be like that a bit more often?" she asked, once she'd finally regained control of herself.

"What?" I asked, genuinely puzzled.

She smiled at me. "Funny," she said, gently poking me in the arm. "Instead of all the chicken jokes."

I shrugged. "The chicken jokes aren't for anyone but me. There's a reason behind them."

"And what is that?" she asked but I shook my head.

"Na-uh," I replied. "I know your name now but we still aren't even."

She tilted her head to one side, a hint of a smile still on her face. "How so?"

"Well... I don't know where you come from. If you want to know why I tell chicken jokes then I want to know why you swan about on your own as an ambassador instead of joining a group."

She stared at me levelly. "I don't know where you come from either! Why are you making such a big deal out of it?"

"Oh." That hadn't occurred to me. Maybe I was just paranoid. "I don't come from around here."

"So where do you come from? And why does it matter?"

We were about halfway down George Street by now, just passing a leafy park-like area. I took a quick look around, pretending to be looking for chickens, but instead taking the time to think about what she'd said.

"I'm from out in the country." I told her after we'd walked a bit further. "From this kind of run-down town called Kemnay. It's pretty isolated. I mean it's big enough. A fair number of shops, an academy and two primary schools. But the buses don't go there that much for some reason. It's like every two hours before you can get into Aberdeen. I was coming in with my brother to see a movie when the attack happened. I lost track of him in the chaos and ended up with the guys at the train station."

"So?" she asked. "Why's that a big deal?"

I shook my head. "I didn't know anyone in town, and they didn't know me. Everyone else knew at least one person in the group from before the attack, but I didn't. I just never felt like I belonged with them. And I miss my brother. It's been a lonely few months."

"You never felt like just trying to get along with them?"

I shook my head again. "You don't understand. I mean, where are you from?"

"Stonehaven."

That was a shock. She was an out-of-towner, like me. "You aren't from around here either? But you know your way around so well. I thought you were an Aberdeen native."

She just smirked at me. "Well some of us haven't been staying in the train station all the time. I spent the winter exploring and trying to find all the groups. Don't blame me for not lying around feeling sorry for myself like you."

I turned away from her, scowling. Then a thought hit me. "Is that why you do it? All the travelling around? You don't know anyone either?"

She didn't answer, just stared ahead, a distant look on her face. "We should stop talking. We're almost there and we don't want to be distracted."

I decided not to push it.

Eventually we turned off George Street and headed towards the Central Library. We climbed the same staircase that I'd gone down with Sam and Mike the day before and walked across the street, our backs to the library. At the base of the stairs I stopped, pretending to catch my breath. The close encounter here with the chicken had only been yesterday. Even though I knew that it was probably long gone part of me expected to find it at the top of the stairs. But there was nothing there. I could see the shopping centre where Argos was. We were getting really close now. One more street and we'd be there.

Rayna looked left and right, as if checking for traffic. I did as well, though I still had no idea what I was actually looking for. She must not have seen anything because she quickly dashed across the road. I followed her, not wanting to be left behind. All of the city was deserted and slightly creepy but now this place felt even worse.

We entered the shopping centre and Rayna gestured inwards. "You go get it," she told me. "I'll stay here and keep watch."

I crept in. It was gloomy, the only light coming in from dirty windows set in the roof. I knew from past visits that Argos was at the back, tucked away to the left. I knew chickens could never get in here, but I kept jumping at every little creak. After passing a couple of deserted stalls I found the shop I was looking for. I had to stop to fish my head torch out of my jacket pocket and tie it on to my forehead. Then I stepped out of the light.

There were no windows in Argos and without electricity the lights were all off. I could only see what was within the small white circle of my torch. It moved as I did, always pointing where I was looking. Occasionally it would streak across the walls as I whipped my head to the side, convinced that I'd seen something moving out of the corner of my eyes. But there was never anything.

I walked behind the counter and entered the storeroom. It was well ordered and I was able to find the TV surprisingly easily. I doubled-checked the number I'd written down from the catalogue and opened the box. The TV was there, small and slim, with a crank on the back to power it. So that was why Glen needed this particular one. He could power it himself. It was a shame I could only take one. I stuffed it in my backpack and headed back.

On the way I passed Waterstones and paused. I thought about what Rayna had said about Glen protecting others and felt a bit of respect for the guy. He was still kind of a jerk, but he looked after his own. It wouldn't hurt to bring some more stuff back for him. Plus, it was likely to sweeten the deal.

I entered the shop and went to the left, where I knew the science fiction section was. I figured that would probably be the sort of thing he was interested in. A title caught my eye and I stopped. It was called *Wings of Bronze*. It must have been quite a big deal because it was on table all of its own, big signs saying 'New Book!'

flapping around it in the breeze from the open door. It actually looked quite interesting, something about airships and robots. I decided to grab one for myself as well. I crammed Glen's copy of *Wings of Bronze* in my rucksack, and stuffed my own copy in my jacket pocket.

Finally, I heaved the rucksack on to my back and started towards the door. Then I stopped, frowning. Rayna was nowhere to be seen. I didn't think she would have wandered off but I couldn't think of any other reason for her not being around. I knew it wasn't a chicken. I'd have heard it coming.

So I walked outside, gently called her name, only to find a white mass standing in front of me. A white mass of people in robes.

CHAPTER 6

A bag was shoved over my head and I was marched swiftly along. Hands gripped my arms tightly and steered me in the direction they wanted me to go, occasionally clutching at me when I stumbled. Occasionally I heard a grunting and one of the group would mutter something. I could just make out Rayna's voice protesting as they hurried us along. At least we were still together. I clenched my fists and started taking deep breaths to calm myself, glad that they couldn't see it through the hood. I'd survived the chickens up to now. I could survive this.

Soon I felt something crunch beneath my feet and realised that I was walking on gravel, not pavement. Not long after that they took me inside somewhere. I stumbled a bit on the stone steps and when I started walking again I could hear my footsteps echoing. Wherever we were, it was big.

Eventually I was shoved into a seat. Rope was wrapped around me and I was bound in place. Footsteps echoed their way away from me and I was alone. I could no longer hear anyone complaining so I figured that they'd taken Rayna with them. It was just me and my imagination. I didn't like that. They'd kidnapped me and now they thought they could just abandon me?

"So...." I started. My voice boomed around me and I stopped for a moment. "That's pretty cool. You get great echoes here. Do you ever try singing?"

I then launched into an off key version of 'Old Man River.' I didn't really like the song but Dad had taught it to me and sung just right it could bounce all over a tunnel in a pretty cool way.

My singing was muffled a bit by the sack and I couldn't really hear properly for the same reason, but it had the desired effect. Before I finished the first verse, the footsteps were back.

"Quiet!" someone snapped at me. I stopped.

"There you are. Do you want to let me see you? Or are you just... chicken?"

I was expecting to be hit or something but I couldn't resist. Besides, they might see my comedy genius and release me. Weirder things had happened.

It certainly made an impression. There was a stunned silence then the voice spoke again.

"You speak wisdom. Please wait for one second. I'll summon the Brotherhood."

He ran off, but sure enough he was back again in a second. And from the way the echoes were bouncing all over the place he'd brought friends. There was a murmuring and then the bag was removed, much more gently then it had been put on. The light hurt my eyes, even though it was dim, and I looked around, blinking, not quite sure what the white shapes were. And then, when my eyes finally did focus, I thought I'd gone mad.

I was in a large church. Light shone in through the stained glass windows, painting bright splashes of colour over the stone walls that surrounded me like a cave. It was an awe-inspiring sight. And it was completely ruined by the weird people who filled it.

Around me were about thirty kids, ranging from a few years younger than me to a few years older. And they were covered in feathers. They'd got white clothes and glued feathers all over them, everywhere they could. Their insane fancy dress project had included making cones of card and wearing them over their faces. I took a quick look at their feet and was confused to see that they were all wearing slippers, the sort that makes your feet look like Godzilla's. Even going by the last few months they were some of the weirdest looking people I'd ever seen.

One of them stepped forward. He'd dyed his hair a brilliant shade of red and gelled it up so that it rose in a giant wave above him, towering over everyone else. He probably needed it because apart from that he was a very weedy boy, probably a year younger than me and even shorter. And when you're shorter than me you've got issues.

I was so shocked by what I was seeing that I couldn't even laugh.

"Welcome, Stranger, to the Brotherhood of the Egg."

I couldn't help it any more. It was too much. I burst out into laughter. There was too much to hold back. It all tried to come out at once and some got caught in my parched throat, so instead of chuckles all I could emit was a weird choking noise. The 'Brotherhood' stared at me for a second, then started doing the same.

The one who had already spoken seemed startled.

"Stranger, who are you that know of our secret tongue?"

By this point I'd run out of air and stopped to get breath. The others continued copying my choking noises, however and the weird sound filled the space.

It was too much to take in so I looked around me, trying to find something I could relate to. That's when I saw Rayna, who was tied to another chair. Apparently they hadn't kept us separate after all. They'd just gagged her.

I jerked my head around questioningly and raised my eyebrows. She just shrugged and rolled her eyes. Whatever was happening, she wasn't impressed. No surprise there then.

"Stranger," the short one said again, bringing my attention back to him. The rest seemed to have calmed down. "Who are you and why do you know so much about us?"

I decided to be serious for once. "I honestly have no idea who you are and I have no clue about any of this."

This caused a brief discussion among the crowd. "Could it be?" one of them yelled. "The chosen one?"

"The chosen one," the rest echoed. Shorty looked around in alarm.

"There's no call for that," he squeaked. "He just got lucky and said the right thing. There's no need to get our feathers ruffled."

The crowd seemed calmed by that. Shorty stared at them for a moment then turned back to me.

"We are the Brotherhood of the Egg," he repeated, seeming annoyed. "We worship our rightful masters who have returned to claim the world."

I'm not the sharpest person in the world (though I might have been the sharpest person in that room) but I guessed what he was meaning. "Chickens?" I asked. "You worship the chickens?"

"The chickens are our masters!" the crowd chorused, flapping their arms and scratching at the ground with their slipper-covered feet. Shorty raised up his arms and screeched into the air.

"Yes, the glorious feathered ones, who have shown us the way!"

I stared at him for a moment. "Chickens?" I repeated.

"The chickens are our masters," the crowd said again, making the gestures. Shorty glared at me.

"Stop that," he told me.

"Stop what?"

"Stop naming them."

"Oh." I raised my eyebrows innocently. "You mean stop saying chickens."

"The chickens are our masters." The crowd did the dance again. It looked like some of them were getting sore arms.

"Yes," Shorty said. "Stop saying chickens."

"The chickens are our masters."

"Oh for feather's sake." He turned away from me for a second. "Our masters like the praise but we don't have to do this every time."

"Yes," I said helpfully, leaning slightly to the side so I could be seen by the crowd. "Let's all stop saying chickens."

"The chickens are our masters!"

"So that's what you do all day?" I asked. "You worship the chic..."

Shorty was faster than I'd given him credit for. He managed to spin away from the crowd and clap a hand across my mouth before I could finish the word. The rest of the group came to a halt and stood meekly, waiting to see what happened next.

"Yes," Shorty hissed, glaring into my eyes. I'd made him angry within five minutes of meeting him. I think that might have been a record. "We worship the feathered ones. Don't use their name lightly, for they are mighty and can crush you. Like a worm."

I shook my head free of his hand and looked around.

"You're all featherbrains," I said, dutifully making the easy pun.

For some reason this seemed to go down well. They all looked at each other and a new murmur rose. Encouraged, I continued.

"I mean, look at you. The Brotherhood of the Egg? More like the Fanatics of Flap."

This one actually got a cheer. I stared at them in confusion. None of my puns or taunts had ever got a cheer before. Mostly people just ignored them. But if I really did have an audience who appreciated my talents then I wasn't going to waste the opportunity.

"I don't know anything about you, but I can figure it all out just by looking. I mean Shorty here is obviously your leader. Tell me, is he in charge just because he fluffed his hair?"

This got a few nods and sniggers, though I couldn't tell if it was because of the fluffed comment or because I'd called their leader Shorty. He obviously didn't like it. With a deep breath he drew himself up and addressed me as sternly as he could.

"My name is Egbert and I am indeed leader here. And you are our prisoner and should stay quiet."

This gave me an idea. I might actually be able to get us out of here.

I copied Egbert and tried straightening a bit, straining against the bonds. The effect was probably about as impressive as it had been on him but I managed to gain an extra inch or two.

"Then shame on you for repeating the mistakes of the humans," I bellowed back at him.

He certainly wasn't expecting that. He just blinked slowly, staring at me. I looked sideways and caught Rayna's eye. She was looking just as confused. I winked at her and continued talking.

"Our chicken masters spent too long locked in cages and now you seek to repeat that suffering? Release my friend and me at once!"

Egbert just laughed but behind him I could see that the rest of the cult were looking at each other. My words had certainly caused confusion, if nothing else. They barely remembered to do the chant and dance at the word 'chickens'.

"And that is not all. You insult them by trying to steal their image."

They stopped talking and just stared at me. Maybe they hadn't understood all the words. Some of them had to be as young as six. To make my point more clear I nodded at their clothes. "What sort of feathers are those? They'd better not be chicken feathers."

Another chorus of "The chickens are our masters!" rolled out before Egbert could stop it. He glared at them angrily before turning back to me. He was good at glaring.

"Of course not. They're from pigeons and craft shops."

I nodded at the slippers. "And what about them? They don't look like chicken feet to me."

He did actually blush a bit at that, his face turning as red as his hair. "Well chi... the feathered ones used to be dinosaurs. So we use dinosaur foot slippers. This is the closest that we could get."

"But they're not quite right, are they? It's nothing to crow about."

I could hear a dull thudding coming from Rayna's direction. By the sound of things she was slowly banging her head against her chair because my puns were so bad. But I was sure I was getting through to them.

"You don't copy their image correctly, but even if you did, do you have the right to strut around dressed like them? Did they give you permission?"

With a desperate glance around Egbert tried to change the subject.

"What we wear is not the issue here. You are."

I would have folded my arms if I could but instead I just tried to look regal. "What is it that you ask of me?" I figured that the new tone would sink in well. And I was right.

"Do you accept the feathered ones as your rightful masters?"

I didn't hesitate. "Of course I do. What sort of an idiot wouldn't?"

The look on his face was priceless. His mouth just sort of gaped open and he seemed completely lost for words. "What did you say?"

"I said of course I do. Look at what they have made of this world. What sense would there be in denying it?"

"But... but... you aren't one of us!" Shorty was really having trouble grasping that I might actually believe his madness. "I've never seen you before."

"And yet I'm here," I replied. "Is it not said that birds of a feather flock together?"

That seemed to go down well. My greatest hope was that they wouldn't realise that I was speaking absolute rubbish.

Egbert looked around. "I don't believe you," he told me, rather stiffly. I just grinned at him.

"For what reason do you not believe me? What have I done that may cause you to think that I feel otherwise about our glorious masters? The chickens?"

"The chickens are our masters!"

I don't think he'd ever had to think about stuff like this before. I had no idea how this whole thing had started but I was pretty sure that not a lot of thought had gone into it.

"Well... why do you believe that they are our masters?" Shorty demanded.

"Because they are unbeatable. The adults have left us behind and now there are only the chickens. Why shouldn't we follow them? I'm not an egghead but I know that much."

"Prove it. Prove you follow them."

I thought frantically then realised something I could use to my advantage. "Look in my jacket pocket. The inside one."

Egbert gave me a suspicious glare, then gestured to

one of his followers, who walked forward nervously. She looked about six and was obviously terrified. I felt sorry for her and gave her an encouraging smile.

"Don't worry," I told her. She smiled back and fished about inside my coat. She soon found the book and pulled it out. "Read the title."

"*Wings of Bronze*," she said, loudly and carefully, then her eyes widened. She dropped the book in my lap and backed away.

"See?" I called loudly. "I even read books about chickens!"

Shorty glanced around in irritation then his eyes fell on Rayna, who he'd apparently forgotten up until now. He pointed triumphantly at her.

"If you are so committed then why did you travel with her? We have seen her before and we know that she is no true friend of the chickens. We know that she seeks their downfall, although they will never be defeated."

That was interesting to know. Shorty's faith in the chickens seemed dependent on them being unbeatable. If Glen really did have a way to beat the chickens then this lot would collapse as well. I filed that away for later use and focused back on the issue at hand.

"I did not know this," I replied. "But what does it matter what she thinks? The chickens are unbeatable. Everyone knows that."

"Everyone but her, apparently. And this is an insult to the chickens. We must give her up to them. Though," and this last bit was obviously said grudgingly, "you seem to have merit, Stranger."

I swallowed, my throat suddenly dry. I remembered Rayna saying that some kids gave people to the chickens. She had almost been caught herself because of it. It certainly explained why she was scared of Union Street. But, more importantly, I could probably get out of this. I would just need to sacrifice Rayna to do it.

"Does she need to be given up? I believe that she can be saved. After all, she did bring me here. Surely that can be counted in her favour? I believe that she needs to be given another chance."

Shorty sneered at me. "Do you indeed? Well you still know little of our ways. So you must make this choice. Do you go with her or do you renounce her and stay?"

I flickered my eyes to the side again but shifted them back when Rayna tried to catch my eyes. Time. I needed more time.

"Well Stranger? What say you?"

"I will give you my answer tomorrow," I said, as loudly and as confidently as I could. "When the rooster gives his call you will know what is on my mind, for that is the proper time for such things."

"Very well." Shorty turned and swept off. I was slightly impressed. I knew it was harder to do a proper sweep than it appears. "Until tomorrow."

Maybe he was expecting his followers to go with him. Some of them did, but most stayed, staring at me.

I knew I'd probably never have this opportunity again as long as I lived so I gave them a great big beaming smile.

"Hey," I said to them. "Want to hear some jokes?"

CHAPTER 7

I managed to keep them entertained for ages. It wasn't easy. There are a lot of chicken jokes in the world but I had to be careful not to say anything that wasn't chicken friendly. To begin with they just stared at me. Eventually, though, one or two of them sniggered then they began to laugh at each one. I tried hard not to show it but it freaked me out a bit. A lot of those jokes weren't even funny.

As hosts they weren't that bad. I mean, we were kept strapped to the chairs for the entire day, which became very uncomfortable very quickly, but we were fed at about lunchtime and again at teatime. They had corn on the cob. I have no idea where they managed to find it, but that's what they gave us. They wouldn't unbind us but they were good enough to hold it so that we could eat. I think they liked me because there was a small argument over who got to feed me. I'm not going to lie, it felt good to be liked. We even got some butter on the corn. I don't know where they got that either.

Eventually night fell and we were left alone. My muscles were all stiff and I really needed to go to the toilet, but at least we were still alive and hadn't been given to the chickens. Rayna hadn't said anything during the whole day, even when they'd taken her gag off so that she could eat. She'd just flexed her mouth one or twice as if trying to work the taste of the gag out of it and taken bites of food. They hadn't replaced it afterwards and she hadn't given them reason to. I think she'd fallen asleep.

"Rayna," I hissed. "Wake up."

"I am awake," she said opening her eyes and straightening her head. "What do you want?"

I frowned at the tone in her voice.

"What is it?" I asked.

She didn't reply for a time and I thought that she really had fallen asleep. Eventually she said, "What are you going to do tomorrow?"

"What?" I asked, momentarily confused.

"What are you going to do tomorrow?" she asked again. "'When the rooster gives his call' as you put it. Are you going to abandon me? Give me up to the chickens?"

"Rayna..."

She wouldn't let me finish. "I wouldn't blame you. You've got to look out for yourself. You hardly know me, after all and you've certainly made it clear that you don't trust me. You even kind of fit in here." Her voice got all choked up and I thought I could see a tear running down her cheek. "Why don't you just look out for number one?"

"Rayna," I said firmly. "Shut up and stop being an idiot."

She looked at me, her mouth hanging open slightly. I was surprised too. I didn't usually speak firmly. "Of course I'm not going to betray you. I just said that to give us some time."

"Time for what?" she asked. I looked at her, worried. How could she not get it?

"Time to escape," I told her. "Are you all right? You really don't seem yourself."

She shook her head. "Of course I'm not all right, idiot. I'm tied to a chair and being held captive by a cult who want to give me to their chicken overlords. Who would be all right with this?"

"OK, OK," I told her, trying to calm her down. "Take a deep breath. Now start from the top. How did they get you? You must have known to look out for them."

She did what I told her, breathing in and trying to compose herself. "Of course I did. But I was looking down towards St Nicholas', where they usually hang out. I didn't know that they would be on one of their pilgrimages. They got me from behind."

I nodded, carefully remembering everything. So we were in the Kirk of St Nicholas. I vaguely remembered it as a tall church. I think I'd been inside it once or twice to look around, but I couldn't remember much about it.

"Their pilgrimage?" I asked. I just had to know.

She nodded wearily. "From time to time they go to a place of evil and throw stuff at it."

"A place of evil? Where?"

"KFC."

I couldn't help it, I cracked up. She glared at me. "Stop it. If you've got a way to get us out of here then do it."

"OK, just give me a second." I started struggling against the ropes that bound me. There had to be a weakness here somewhere.

After fifteen minutes, I realised that there wasn't. For all their silliness, someone in the Brotherhood of the Egg must have been in the Scouts or something because these were really well tied knots. I tried rocking the chair backwards and forwards but it was old and heavy and wouldn't budge. Twenty minutes after that I finally accepted it. There was no way out.

"Any luck?" Rayna asked. I knew that she'd been doing the same thing. From the defeat in her voice she hadn't had any more success than I had.

"Um... no. But I'm sure that something will come up."

She didn't even reply to that, just snorted. I knew that it was hopeless as well. The only one who knew where we were was Glen and he wasn't likely to notice that we were gone or care if he did. He'd probably just assume that we weren't to be trusted after all. Even if someone from the train station knew they probably wouldn't do anything about it. We had a rule that said that if someone didn't come back then that was it. It was easier just believing that they'd left of their own accord than because they'd been caught.

There was no one coming to save us.

"So what are you going to do?" Rayna asked after a while. "What are you going to do tomorrow? When they ask for your decision?"

I thought about it for a moment. "I don't know," I said honestly.

"You don't know? What is there to know? Either you save yourself or you give us both to the giant chickens."

The despair in her voice was horrible to hear.

"Well what do you want me to do?" I asked.

"I don't want to be taken. I really don't." She said it in a little voice that made my insides curl up. I had to do something.

"What day of the week do chickens hate the most?"

There was a pause. "What?"

"I said what day of the week do chickens hate the most?"

"Why are you asking me that now?" I could hear a hint of anger creeping into her voice. Good.

"Fry-day. Why did the chick disappoint his mother?"

"Seriously, shut up with the chicken jokes." She was definitely getting more annoyed.

"Because he wasn't everything he was cracked up to be. What do you get when a chicken lays an egg on a hill?"

She began to rock backward and forwards in her chair, though it didn't move. "Shut up, shut up, shut up!"

I delivered the punch line. "An eggroll."

And from the shadows off to our left came a giggle.

We both froze. "Who's there?" I called.

Out of the shadows crept the little girl who had taken the book out of my jacket. All day she'd been sitting in the front row of the crowd, gazing up at me. Now she was back.

And she had a knife.

I instantly fixed my eyes on it. "What are you doing?" I asked, trying to appear calm.

The girl circled round behind me. I tried turning my head to keep up with her but eventually she passed the point where my head wouldn't turn any more. I held my breath, not sure what was about to happen. Then there was a brief sawing sound and my hands were free.

It felt amazingly good. I could only groan as she went to work on the rope stretched around my chest. When that finally gave way I almost fell forward. I managed to catch myself just in time and massaged my wrists, trying to get some feeling into them. I regretted it a moment later as pain flared sharply through them, but it was better than the numbness. I looked at them and saw that the ropes had left impressions around each hand. I quickly looked away again. The sight just brought more pain.

While I'd been tending to my hands the girl had freed my legs, which also started hurting a moment later. I tried to stand up but collapsed back down again. It would take a lot of stretching before my legs were able to support my weight. I turned to the girl and did my best to smile through the pain.

"Could you go and free that girl over there?" I asked, pointing. She looked up at me solemnly, then nodded and scampered over to Rayna, carrying the knife with exaggerated care. A moment later the sound of her hacking away at the ropes drifted over.

I began jerking and kicking my legs, trying to wake them up. Now that we were free I didn't want to wait around any longer than I had to. *Wings of Bronze* had fallen off my lap onto the floor at some point during the day and I picked it up, tucking it back inside my jacket. It might have just saved my life. The least I could do was actually read it.

After about five minutes I was able to get up and totter over to Rayna, who was only just getting feeling back into her legs herself. She looked up at me and I saw relief flit across her face. "We're going to be fine," she whispered. I just nodded to her.

"Let's go before they notice that we're free." She tried to heave herself up but I pushed her back down.

"Give it another few minutes. I want to try something."

I turned to the little girl and held out my hand. "Can I have the knife, please?"

She nodded and handed it to me. I don't know where she'd got it but it was a vicious thing, with a serrated blade on one edge. It looked like it had come from a survival shop to be used against bears or something. I carefully put it to one side and began gathering up all the cut rope. "Do you know where they put our bags?" I asked her.

She nodded again and skipped off, a white ghost in the darkness. A second later she was back dragging my bag. I coiled the rope and was putting it inside when she returned again with Rayna's bag.

"What are you doing?" asked Rayna, still sitting there. I looked up at her and winked.

"Sowing some confusion," I told her and pulled out my notebook. "See I use this to jot down chicken jokes when there's no one there to tell them to. It's great when I'm on watch with nothing to do." I tore out one of the pages. It hurt a bit to do it. I'd got really attached to the notebook and vandalising it like that didn't feel quite right. But part of me felt that the spirit of the notebook knew what I was doing and would have agreed. I dug a pen out of a pocket and scribbled on the piece of paper. Then I held it up for Rayna to see.

"'We've flown the coop,'" she read out loud. Then she focused on me. "Really?"

I shrugged as the little girl beside me giggled. "It's worth a try. Now let's go." I turned to the girl. "Coming?"

"What?" Rayna and the girl said it at the same time. I looked at Rayna and shrugged.

"Well, we can't leave her here. She might get into trouble. And she did help us."

"But she's one of them."

"She's a human," I said firmly. I could tell that Rayna wasn't thinking clearly. The joy of being free combined with the fear she still felt was a confusing mixture. "That means she's one of us."

Then I turned to the girl. "Do you want to come with us?" I asked her, holding out a hand. She thought about it for a moment, then took my hand and nodded. I reached out my other hand to Rayna and helped pull her to her feet. We got our backpacks firmly settled then set off, creeping down the pews. Luckily we'd been kept near the doors and we didn't have to go through any side rooms to get out. Rayna eased the door open and we stepped out into the night.

We were still unsteady on our feet and the little girl looked exhausted. I guess she wasn't used to late nights. The air was crisp and cold. I knew we couldn't go far, but we needed to get far enough away that we could take shelter and not be found when they eventually came after us. I was tempted to head for the train station but I couldn't be sure that we'd make it. The last thing that I wanted to do was lead the cult back there. So I made for the top of Upperkirkgate and the Aberdeen College building. There was a museum we should be able to get in through, and it was a big enough building that we'd probably be able to escape out of a side door if we needed to.

We made it most of the way there when the bells in the church behind us began pealing out. We lurched forward faster, all three of us dead on our feet. I remembered going up to the top of the church tower once and seeing a little piano that controlled the bells. That was the only way to explain what I was hearing.

"What is that?" Rayna asked while I began to chortle.

The little girl looked up and said, deadpan, "That's the warning bells."

Rayna frowned down at her. "It's the Birdie Dance song."

I burst out into laughter. "Oh, Egbert's group is the best."

Rayna shot me an angry glare and together we staggered into the museum and to safety.

CHAPTER 8

We crept through the museum and into Aberdeen College itself, finally finding a coffee room with comfortable looking couches. The little girl walked over to one and curled up without saying a word, falling asleep quickly. Rayna and I grabbed a couch each. It might have been the adrenaline of our close escape, but we just lay there, staring wide-eyed at the ceiling.

Rayna was the first to break the silence. "What would you have done?" she asked.

I really didn't want this conversation, but Rayna wasn't likely to drop it any time soon. So I sighed and said, "I don't know."

"You don't know?" Her voice was perfectly smooth, like quicksand. I had a feeling that I had to tread carefully during this conversation or I'd find myself in deep trouble.

"No, I don't know. I want to say that I would have said that we couldn't be separated, but I don't know if that's true. I might have cracked at the last moment. Like an egg."

"Stop that," she said, her voice a harsh whip crack. The little girl stirred slightly in her sleep and we didn't say a thing until she had calmed down. Eventually I spoke again.

"Look, I'm sorry. I don't know what to tell you. But it's the truth and at least it's better that than a lie."

There was the sound of her releasing her breath, slowly, like a balloon deflating. "That's fair, I guess. I'm sorry, I was just so scared back there."

I nodded up at the ceiling. "Yeah, me too."

"No you weren't," she corrected me. "I was watching you all day. You were just sitting there, cracking jokes without a care in the world. I don't know if you're really brave or really stupid but you don't seem to be afraid of anything. I guess... I guess I kind of envy you that."

"Don't bother," I told her. "I spend most of the time terrified. I could hardly think straight for fear."

"What do you mean?"

I guess it was time for the truth. She still hadn't told me that much about herself but right then I didn't care. Maybe it made me weak, but she was the closest thing to a friend I had in this world.

"I don't make jokes because I'm brave. I make them because I'm really, really scared."

There was a brief moment of silence. Then she went, "Oh," drawing out the O to show that she understood.

I spelt it out anyway. It felt good to just be honest.

"I mean, look around us. We're in an apocalypse

caused by chickens. Or giant chicken shaped things anyway. How can anyone take that seriously? I mean, if I actually stopped and thought about it, about how giant robot things are stalking the streets, I'd probably just collapse and cry. How can we even take those things on? They're bigger than tanks, their beaks can peck through concrete and they lay explosive eggs. So I make jokes. Especially about chickens. I refuse to take it seriously. It's just my coping mechanism. It probably helps that I've never actually seen anyone taken. I can pretend it's as stupid as I want. So there you go. There's the big secret. I'm actually a huge coward."

I let out a huge breath. She now knew all my 'secrets'; everything important about me in this new world. It was scary but also kind of nice. Even if I hadn't traded a secret for a secret like I had wanted to.

Then she began to talk.

"I actually lived just outside Stonehaven, on a farm. A chicken farm. And I was there the day that the chickens came."

I blinked up at the ceiling. She had lived on a chicken farm? I couldn't even begin to imagine what the chickens would have done about that.

She kept on talking. "The day started normally. I'd helped to feed the chickens with Dad. I remember that they all seemed unusually alert but I didn't think anything of it at the time. I was getting ready to go into town. Then there was this noise like a plane getting closer and closer. I hurried outside and saw these giant shapes coming right towards us. I yelled to my family and everyone else came piling out. My mum, my dad and my little sister, Hazel, who was two years younger than me."

I did the maths in my head. That would have made Hazel a year younger than me. Eleven.

"We didn't know what it was but we knew it was bad. We all ran towards the car but Dad wanted to make sure the chickens were all locked up first. He was just coming out of the barn when a chicken landed right in our front garden. Did you say that you'd seen their laser eyes?"

I nodded. I'd seen them in action.

"Well, it swung its head around and took the top right off the barn, like it was cutting open a packet of cereal or something. It was between Dad and us so he just yelled at us to go, backing away towards the house. It seemed more interested in him and we managed to get away.

"We had no idea what to do. We just drove toward Aberdeen. Mum made us try and call the police or something but none of our mobiles would work. Then we got to Aberdeen just as the chickens hit there."

There was a catch in her voice and I knew she was crying. I didn't say anything and just let her get on with her story. Interrupting now would be wrong.

"It was like something out of a nightmare. It's still in my nightmares. We got to the police station and a rush of people came at us. We all got separated in the crowd.

I ended up hiding in a house somewhere. I don't know where. I guess Mum must have got taken along with everyone else because I haven't seen her or any other adult since. I searched and searched for my little sister."

She didn't talk for a long while. Eventually I had to prompt her.

"Did you ever find her?"

"Yeah," she said, swallowing a sob. "On Union Street."

And now everything made sense.

"She'd fallen in with the Egbert's lot. I tried talking to her, to make her see sense. I think that I was getting through to her because the next thing I knew Egbert had turned her over to the chickens. I still see it, Jesse. I can still see the Brotherhood coming for us, trying to grab us. Hazel just calmly told me to go and then she walked over to them. A chicken was already there. They formed a circle around, made sure that she couldn't get away. She didn't even try. She was just frozen to the spot, terrified. The chicken leaned down, looking at her through first one eye then the other. Then it just pecked down and grabbed her. If you look carefully I'm sure you can still see the mark its beak gorged into the concrete. And she was gone. I couldn't do a thing."

The last word ended with another sob.

"Later I learned all about the Brotherhood. The chickens use them for guarding and keeping an eye out for troublesome kids. They give them food and leave them be, as long as they do what they want."

She swallowed, obviously gathering her thoughts and trying to calm down. "A couple of days after they took Hazel I found a guy who said that he'd been captured by the chickens but managed to escape. They'd taken him to the Pittodrie football stadium down by the beach and put him in a cage with some other kids they'd caught. I went to take a look for myself, hoping that I could find her, but the security was too good. The Brotherhood was all over it. And I couldn't ask the guy who escaped for more information because the chickens got him again. They have a way of tracking down anyone who escapes. My sister didn't stand a chance. And then I realised something. It wasn't that I was weak. The chickens were just too strong. There was nothing I could do on my own."

She raised her head and looked at me. Even in the dark I could see the gleam in her eye.

"But all of us together? We have a chance. That's why I don't join anyone. Why I'm so set on getting everyone together so that we can take the chickens down. To pay them back for what they did to me and my family."

Rayna didn't speak after that. I wanted to go over and give her a hug, just to let her know that it was all going to be OK but I felt too awkward. Hugs were something mums gave.

So I said what I could.

"You know, people reckon that the Catchers don't kill kids when they get taken. If they wanted to kill them it would be easier to do it where they are, instead of taking them off somewhere else. I saw plenty of lasers being fired when they first attacked, but I never saw them hit anyone. They just destroyed some buildings and some roads. So I think that it's pretty safe to say that your sister is still alive. And if that's the case, we will get her back."

She turned her head and I could see a tiny bit of hope in her eyes as she looked at me. "Yeah?"

"You better believe it. I'm not getting beaten by some overgrown feather duster."

She chuckled slightly. "So we've both learned a lot about each other tonight," she whispered. I nodded in agreement, though I knew she couldn't see me.

"I promise not to tell anyone that you are obsessed with beating the chickens because of your family."

"And I promise not to tell anyone that you only make chicken jokes because you're scared. But... uh... could you do me a favour? Your chicken jokes are still really, really annoying. So could you please try and dial them down a bit?"

I smiled at her. "I promise to try."

CHAPTER 9

I woke up the next morning to find the little girl staring down at me, wide-eyed and silent. She was still wearing her cult outfit and looked very creepy. I started and jerked away from her. She seemed shocked and did the same thing.

"Sorry, but you gave me quite the surprise there," I told her, glancing over at Rayna. She was still asleep and I decided to leave her like that. I hadn't found yesterday pleasant but it had to have been even worse for her. "What's your name?"

"Henny," she said, in a little voice as clear as a bell. I frowned at her and got to my feet.

"Is that your real name?" I asked her. She thought about it for a second then slowly shook her head. "What is your real name?"

"It's Lizzie," she told me. I smiled down at her.

"Well Lizzie, how would you like something to eat?"

She almost tore the cereal bar that I offered her out of my hand and ripped off the wrapping before stuffing it in her mouth. I guess having corn on the cob every day wasn't that satisfying.

I left her with another cereal bar and told her to watch Rayna while I went to explore. I was hoping that I could find some other clothes for the little girl. I was getting uneasy around that costume she was wearing. But I was out of luck.

I did manage to find a vending machine. Vending machines were like treasure chests in our world. Usually they just taunted anyone who found them. It was almost impossible to break the glass quietly and it was always possible that a chicken could hear you if you did. Since there was no electricity any more we couldn't even steal money to pay for the chocolate inside. But I'd managed to find a vending machine key a couple of months ago, so I was able to open any that I came across. I didn't let others know that I had it. It was probably the most precious thing that I owned, which was pretty sad when you came to think about it.

I walked back to the room with my pockets filled with bars of chocolate. When I got in I found Rayna staring at Lizzie suspiciously, while the little girl sat as far away from her as possible. What was needed here was something to diffuse the atmosphere, but I'd already promised to lay off the chicken jokes. (Get it?)

Instead all I had was mindless chatter.

"I quite like being back here," I said as I got in. "It reminds me of home."

Lizzie looked up at me with wide eyes. "You used to live in a castle?"

I laughed and shook my head, knocking a hand against a nearby wall. "No, but it's made of stone from near where I live. See this? Kemnay granite. A lot of things in this city are made of it. It's nice to be reminded of where I come from."

I handed out some of my vending machine loot and Lizzie grabbed at hers with a shriek of delight. Rayna ate hers more slowly, savouring the taste. Then she looked at me with what looked like interest.

"They seriously took granite all the way from Kemnay to build this?"

I sighed. "That's nothing. There's stuff built from Kemnay granite all around the world. The parliament building in Edinburgh has some in it. So does the Cenotaph in London. And the Sydney Harbour bridge."

Lizzie looked up at me then the walls, her eyes wide. "Wow."

"Do you know where Sydney is, Lizzie?"

She snorted, apparently disgusted that I'd even asked the question. "Of course I do. It's in Australia. We have a map of the world in our classroom at school. I'm not a stupid baby."

"Sorry," I told her, chucking her another chocolate bar. "My mistake."

"How do you know all that?" Rayna asked me, while Lizzie tore into her prize. I groaned.

"I didn't want to. I had this teacher in school who was obsessed with all of that. Said we should be proud of our cultural heritage. I'd have been prouder if the village had a swimming pool."

After that Rayna got some cans out of her pack and we feasted on more cold soup. I made sure that none of them were chicken. It was probably better to ease Lizzie gently into stuff like that. Which reminded me...

"Lizzie, why did you help us yesterday?" I asked her. She looked up from her vegetable soup, a look of simple contentment on her face.

"You seemed nice. And you told funny jokes. I didn't want you to get hurt. So I waited until everyone else was asleep then I stole Egbert's knife and rescued you."

"Well I'm really glad you did. My name is Jesse and this is Rayna. Do you want to come along with us now?"

She thought for a second then nodded. "Yes."

"Good. Now we'll be walking for quite a long way today. Do you think you can handle that?"

She nodded again. "Yes, I can."

"Good. Now why don't you go to the toilet before we set off? It's just down the hall."

She turned and darted out the door.

"What do you think?" I asked Rayna quietly. She just shrugged.

"Well we've got her now, for better or for worse, though you know she'll just slow us down."

"Yeah," I agreed. "But I think it's the only thing to do."

"Besides," Rayna added. "They got my sister. They're not getting this little one. We've just got to be careful. She's been with the Brotherhood for a couple of months now. It will be hard to undo that."

"But we will," I said. There was no point in telling Rayna that I'd already started thinking of Lizzie a bit like a little sister. I'd always wanted a little sister. And this felt like fighting back against the chickens in some strange way. We weren't giving up and we were sticking together. It seemed like the most important thing we could do for our future.

Lizzie didn't hold us back as badly as I thought she would, but she soon began complaining that her feet were hurting. I wasn't really surprised. Her slippers probably did well on the worn floors of the church but they weren't really practical for outside use. Luckily by this point we were close to the Morrisons I'd spotted earlier so we ducked in for a quick spot of looting. We were able to get Lizzie to exchange her chicken outfit for some more normal clothes and shoes quite easily. We also gave her a backpack with a change of clothes and some cereal bars in it. Then we left again, back on King Street.

It took longer than it had before because we kept an eye on Lizzie and stopped every time it looked like she was flagging. It was late in the day before we finally arrived back at the University Library. Glen looked quite surprised to see us, and even more surprised to see Lizzie.

"I asked you to bring me back a TV, not a brat," were his first words on seeing all of us. Lizzie behaved in a more civilised manner and merely stuck her tongue out at him.

"Calm down, we've got your stupid TV." I hauled it out of the bag and handed it to him. He took it, with a gleeful expression.

"Finally. Oh, you have no idea how long I've been waiting for this." He was so happy he was almost dancing with delight.

Rayna stepped forward, all official Ambassadorness. "We've upheld our end of the bargain and proved that we can be trusted. Now give us what we want."

Glen was distracted and for a moment I thought that he hadn't heard what we'd said. "What? Oh, the way to defeat the chickens."

"What?" Lizzie hissed, shocked. "But you can't defeat the chickens."

"If we can't, then there's no point in worrying about what he's got to say, is there?" I reasoned. She frowned and then nodded.

Glen stared at her, unsure for a moment. Rayna snapped her fingers in front of his eyes. "Focus. What's the way?"

"Uh? Oh. Right. Well, naturally the first question you'll be asking yourself is, why chickens?"

Rayna and I looked at each other and I shrugged.

"You know, I hadn't actually thought about that." I said.

"Seriously?" Glen looked shocked. "That's the first thing that came to mind. I mean, it's not something you'd expect to happen, is it?"

"Well I always just assumed that they were robots or aliens that were posing as chickens for some reason."

"Nope, it's chickens. There are chickens inside each of the Catchers, wired in somehow. Trust me, I've seen it."

Well this was news; we really were fighting chickens. The very fact that he could have claimed to see inside one of the robots was pretty astonishing. But it wasn't really worth all the food he was asking for.

"Anything else, Doc?"

He looked absurdly pleased with the nickname for some reason and nodded. "Oh yes, much more. I think I might have found out why they're so smart."

"So this isn't just natural?"

He looked at me like I was an idiot. "Don't be stupid. They're chickens."

"Not alien chickens?"

"They're not aliens. They're perfectly ordinary chickens."

"Then who's controlling them? They must have a leader?"

Rayna butted in. "Yeah, if they're just chickens then they must have someone telling them what to do."

Glen growled exasperatedly. "I don't know who's leading them. I don't know why they're doing this. I just know that they're ordinary chickens that can somehow control massive robots."

"So something made them smarter?"

He raised a finger and waggled it at me. "Exactly. And I think I've found what."

He beckoned us towards a flight of stairs leading up. I told Lizzie to stay down on this floor, and followed Glen. Rayna was close behind me.

We emerged on to the wide flat roof of the library building. Someone, presumably Glen, had tied a rope to the last rung of the steps and we all clung onto it. Maybe it was just me, but I'd seen too many movies which involved people sliding on ice into some sort of chasm to be comfortable up here. Glen led us over to a mast and pointed at the box at its base. For some reason it was covered in tinfoil.

"Do you have to keep it warm?" I asked, loudly.

He started unwrapping it. "No," he bellowed. "It's to block signals. I don't want the chickens tracking them back to me."

As the last of it was pulled away the screen on the box lit up.

"You see that?" He yelled. "There's the proof."

He flicked a switch and I could see a number of wavy lines appear on the screen.

"What does it mean?" Rayna yelled back at him. I was pleased to see that it wasn't just me who didn't understand.

"It's... oh hang on, let's just go back inside."

Very thankful, I led the way back and was surprised at the quiet inside the library. The wind must have been louder than I had thought.

"It's a carrier wave," Glen said after we had grabbed a seat at a nearby table. Lizzie was napping in a corner. "I think that it's sending instructions to the chickens and making them very smart."

"That's it? That there's some sort of weird signal in the air? We went traipsing all the way over Aberdeen, went through all that, just for a signal?"

Glen looked slightly bemused at my annoyance. "What's the big deal? You only had to get a TV."

I growled at him but Rayna placed a hand on my shoulder, like last time, and gave it a warning squeeze.

"So the chickens are all being controlled by this signal?" she asked. "What happens when the signal gets cut out?"

"Without the signal they can't operate. If they can't operate then they're just chickens stuck in a big metal shell," Glen said.

Now I got it. "So all we have to do is to cut off the signal and they're useless? The chickens all fall over or explode or something?"

He nodded. "Sort of. They'll probably still be able to control their machines, but they won't have the intelligence to pose a threat. If you went at them they'd probably run away."

"Who's sending the signal?" I asked.

His smile faded. "I don't know."

"You don't know?"

"Well, it was pretty lucky that I was able to find the signal in the first place," he said defensively. "It just happened by chance. I haven't been able to do anything more with it than identify it. I would have to leave the University and wander about to triangulate the signal."

"All right," I said, getting to my feet. "Grab your stuff and let's go."

He shied away from me. "No way. I'm not leaving."

"That's what you think," I said, taking another step towards him. I was still holding out hope that he could just be intimidated into doing it, but Rayna restrained me again.

"No, leave it, Jesse. If he doesn't want to go then we can't make him. Now sit back down."

I did, grumbling and shooting Glen hostile glances. He seemed very flustered. Good.

"Look, even if I wanted to go with you I probably couldn't," he said. "I don't have the stuff I need. This is a university, not an FBI outpost or something. And even if we did have it I'm not sure I would know how to use it. I only managed to get that because I was trying to see if there were any TV stations still transmitting."

"Why were you looking?" I asked.

"I thought there might be some emergency channels still working, maybe some government broadcasts."

I looked up, hopeful. "Anything?"

He shook his head. "Every so often there seem to be things broadcast, but I've not been able to see them. That's what I was wanting the TV for. Anything to help us survive."

I looked at him, interested. If there was a chance of picking up a broadcast, maybe the Train Station Gang would have to get a TV for themselves.

I went and got the book I'd picked up. "Here," I told a surprised Glen. "I figured that since I was in the area anyway I'd pick up a book for you. I hope I got what you liked."

He looked at the book and I swear I could see tears swelling in his eyes. "Thanks. Thank you very much."

"No problem," I said, looking away and feeling uncomfortable. "Just since I was in the area anyway. It wasn't any skin off my nose."

"Look, I'm really sorry I can't help you," he blurted out. "But I could probably narrow it down. I'm sure the signal isn't coming from a satellite and I'm also pretty sure that they're not using the mobile phone networks. It would have to be some sort of signal mast. They've probably got them set up in every place they invaded. I don't know if that helps at all."

It did... a bit. At least we knew that if it was a local signal we stood a chance of destroying it. If the source of the signal was on the ground it would mean that we only had to blow up an antenna or something. Though I had no idea how we'd be able to do that either.

"So all we have to do is find out where the signal is coming from, then stop it somehow?"

Rayna looked a bit grim as well. It wasn't going to be an easy task, but the look on her face told me that she was resolute. "We'll do it somehow. Thanks, Glen, for everything. I'll make sure you get paid."

He nodded uncertainly. "You can stay here for the night," he said, gesturing around. I looked at Rayna hopefully. I didn't really want to walk all the way to the sofa shop again. Night was only about an hour away and I didn't want to risk meeting whatever might be lurking out there. She shrugged and nodded.

We had tea together. I'm not sure if Glen really was covering for anyone, but if he was then he didn't go to see them that night. The meal was a tense affair. Glen seemed uncomfortable with our presence and seemed to want to escape to his TV and books as soon as possible. Rayna was glum, probably looking ahead at the huge task in front of us.

"So what do we have to do?" I said to Rayna while Lizzie slurped away happily. "To defeat the chickens. If we make a rough plan now then it'll be easier to know what to do."

Rayna leaned towards me slightly, staring intently. "What do you mean we?"

"Oh." Right. I was only supposed to be along for negotiations with Glen. After this I'd be going right back to the train station. I really didn't want to. I wasn't exactly enjoying having to walk for hours, dodging giant birds and mad chicken cults, but it beat lying on my bed back home.

"Well I just thought that it would be better if we didn't bring Lizzie so close to her old home. I mean if she ever ran away then it would be easy enough for her to lead them there. And I can't just leave her with you. It wouldn't be fair." Beside me Lizzie hummed in agreement. "Do you not want me around?"

Rayna cast her head back arrogantly, but smiled at me while she did it. "I guess I've got used to you hanging around," she replied.

I smiled. "So what do we need? First we find the signal. Then what?"

She shrugged. "We'll need an army to take it down. And then we'll have to actually attack it. Once it's down... I guess none of us know what will happen after that."

I nodded and thought that the next few months wouldn't be that bad. Travelling around Aberdeen, trying to work out where the signal was coming from. When it was actually time to do something about it then it would be terrifying. But for the moment I was pleased with the job I had in front of me.

Then Glen had to come and ruin it all.

"I've got it," he said, hurrying over, his eyes shining. "I think I know what's transmitting the signal."

Suddenly Rayna was all business again. "What?" she asked. "Tell me."

"Aberdeen used to have a broadcasting house as part of the BBC. I bet that it's there. I think it was working on the same frequencies. And it would be powerful enough to cover the city."

"Do you know where it is?" Rayna asked urgently.

Glen nodded. "Yeah, it's just off Beechgrove Terrace. I think that's where they originally filmed that gardening show – the Beechgrove Garden."

Rayna nodded. "There's a high chicken presence around that area. I've never been able to get close to it. But it would make sense." She looked out the window, where the sun was slowly setting. "We'll have to go and check it out, just to make sure."

I followed her gaze, then it hit me. "You don't mean now, do you?"

"Of course not," she said. I just had time to relax before she added. "It's not dark enough. We'll leave in an hour."

I took a step back from the window. I hadn't been out at night for months. Not since the whole thing had begun. "Are you sure it's safe?"

"It'll be easier to sneak up on them at night. Besides," and here she hesitated for a moment, "this way we'll be able to avoid any trouble."

I said, "What?" at about the same time Glen muttered, "Cody."

I turned to him and stared. "Who's Cody?" I asked.

"Someone you don't want to meet." He replied. Before I could question him more Rayna butted in.

"Can you look after Lizzie for us while we're away, Glen?"

He nodded, though he didn't look happy. "Of course. But look, Rayna. Whatever you find there... just be careful, OK?"

CHAPTER 10

I'd never really had a problem with the dark before the chicken apocalypse. Kemnay is right out in the country and sometimes Dad would take me out late at night to go star-gazing. The air would be crisp and my breath would form clouds in front of my face. We'd go up the nearest hill where the lights from the town wouldn't block out the night sky. It always took my breath away.

But this dark was different. This time I didn't have Dad standing next to me, holding my hand. Now I only had Rayna and the threat of chickens in the dark.

She took us up a different street to the one we had arrived in. We had been walking for only five minutes when I realised I had no idea where we were. Everything was different in the dark. The retail park we passed was like a deep pit, just waiting for us to fall in. The railway line after that was like a river. I moved so I was walking a bit closer to Rayna and hoped that she didn't notice.

Further on into the night we trudged, through a maze of streets. Finally we were on a better road;

there was only a park on one side. On the other side was a solid line of houses. It didn't last long, though. Another crossroads and we left them behind. I could almost feel ghosts in windows behind us, waving us goodbye. I began to shiver. But there, in the distance, was some light. The street lights were on, showing the empty road ahead.

Rayna saw the lights as well and stopped. "Is that where we're heading?" I asked her.

I could just make out her shaking her head. "We've still got a few streets to go. We'll... what is it?"

I'd grabbed her arm and hauled her over to the side of the road, putting my hand over her mouth. The vibrations that I'd felt grew worse and then the chicken appeared from the right side of the crossroad. It didn't pause, just turned down the lit street and kept walking.

As soon as it was gone Rayna shook me off. "You didn't have to grab me," she said, her voice angry. "You could have just said."

"Sorry," I replied, my eyes still focused on where the chicken had gone. "I didn't want to take the chance that it might hear me."

"Well fine," she said, her voice slightly less annoyed. "I guess it's OK if you..."

I felt another chicken coming and grabbed her again. She elbowed me in the ribs, but stayed still and quiet until it had come and gone, following exactly the same path as the first one. "Next time, just tap me on the shoulder," she said, her voice a growl. I just nodded.

"That's two," I said, my voice shaking slightly. "I've not seen any together since the first attack."

She was about to reply when I tapped her shoulder. A third chicken appeared and disappeared, exactly like the others. "What are they doing?" I murmured.

Rayna turned and looked at me, her eyes shining. "They're patrolling," she whispered back. "Glen must have been right. There's something important to them here."

"But if they're patrolling like that, how are we going to get in and check it out?"

"We'll have to wait until we see a gap, then hide in someone's garden to get closer."

Twenty chickens later and we sat panting on the grass, a wall pressed against our back. The chickens had been going by like clockwork and there had been a gap of only a few seconds to dash across the road and vault a high wall, which we'd got over by climbing on some bins. Another two chickens passed by us before we got our breath back enough to speak.

"How many chickens do you think they have here?" I asked.

She shook her head. "Not sure. First let's find where the signal is coming from. Then we'll worry about how to get past the chickens."

We began making our way forward, scrambling over walls and freezing any time we thought we heard a noise. The darkness had terrified me on the way here, but now I wished it would come back. All the street lights were on and we ducked between shadows when we could. After about ten minutes Rayna nudged me and pointed. I followed her finger and saw a massive TV mast poking out above the surrounding houses.

"Is that it?" I asked. She shrugged.

"If Glen is right then yes, I think so. We're going to have to get closer though. Come on."

I didn't move, just stared at it. "It's huge," I said. "How are we supposed to take it down?"

"Jesse!" Rayna snapped her fingers in front of my face. "One thing at a time. Let's get there first."

I shook myself out of it. "OK. If we get into one of the houses over there we should be able to see it properly."

In the streetlight her teeth glowed orange when she grinned. "OK, let's do it."

It was another tense ten minutes, but finally we made it to one of the houses by the antenna. The back door was unlocked and we let ourselves in, careful not to leave any sign of our presence. The inside of the house was totally dark and I almost walked into a table. We managed to make our way upstairs and found two bedrooms.

"We should sleep here tonight," Rayna said. "Then check out the security tomorrow."

The idea of spending the night in a house so close to so many chickens would normally have scared me half to death but it had been a long day. At the very mention of sleep I felt a blanket of tiredness drop over me, blocking out any fear.

"All right, see you in the morning," I said.

Tired as I was, it would be hours before I could actually get to sleep. The stomping of the chickens going past outside kept jerking me awake and when I finally did begin to slumber the chickens marched straight from reality into my dreams.

I was woken the next morning by Rayna putting her hand over my mouth. I'm fairly sure she did it as a kind of revenge because when I woke up panicking she just grinned at me. Shrugging her off, I swung my feet out of bed and accepted the breakfast bar she gave me.

"What have I missed?" I asked between bites.

"Come and see," she replied, her voice grim. She grabbed my arm, pulling me over to the window. I looked out and my heart sank.

The chickens had turned the place into a fortress.

Beechgrove Terrace might have been a nice place in a different time. There were trees and I could see some lawns and things. But you couldn't ignore the chickens. There was one of the Catchers standing in the car park, idly perched on the dented bonnet of a red Ford. Even as I watched, another Catcher thumped past on the road on the other side of the building. The mast towered over everything. I could just see its base. And, more importantly, I could see what was next to it. A green wooden gate led into an area protected by yellow warning signs covered with black lightning bolts. Behind it I thought I could see some machinery, like a generator or something. That must be important. If we could smash that up, maybe it would cut off this signal.

"Rayna..." I tugged her sleeve and pointed towards the area, but she'd already seen it.

"Look closer," she said and passed me some binoculars.

I put them up to my eyes and twiddled the nobs. I could see something moving down there, but it wasn't until I got the binoculars to focus that I saw what it was.

Before, when I'd heard rumours about other types of chickens, I'd asked myself what else the chickens could need if they had giant metal robot chickens. I got my answer here.

Smaller chickens, just a little bigger than normal size. Their metal skins glinted in the weak sunlight and it looked like they were wearing robotic suits. Their eyes gleamed green and they marched back and forth, obviously guarding the area.

We crept away from the window so we wouldn't be seen. My heart was pounding.

"Why did the robot cross the road?" I asked.

"I don't know, why did the robot cross the road?"

"Because the chicken was out of order."

She groaned but I thought I saw her smile a bit.

"So what do we do now?" I asked.

The hint of that smile disappeared. "We'll keep watch for the day and try and see if we can spot any weaknesses in their defence. Then we get out of here and work out what to do."

"Rayna, this is crazy. We can't do anything here. We had no idea there were so many of them. And we don't even know what those chicken commandos can do."

The smile was back again. "Chicken commandos?"

I shrugged. "That's what I'm calling the smaller ones. It seems fitting."

"I guess." Rayna thumped me on the shoulder. "Well look, we're stuck here for the rest of the day anyway. It can't hurt to just look."

I wasn't so sure. There was something about Rayna, some echo in her voice, that unnerved me. I just couldn't quite put my finger on it.

But there was no arguing with her. "OK," I said. "Just one day."

It was worth it. Rayna borrowed my notebook and filled page after page with detailed notes about the chickens' positioning, timing and movements. We spent most of the morning creeping around the house, peeking out of windows. Rayna had worked out that there were four chickens patrolling the perimeter, recognising one with a scratched wing and then counting until it came round again. However, I was the one who saw the other guards.

At first it was just a flash of white out of the corner of my eye. It was my turn with the binoculars and I was able to take a quick look. Then I'd scuttled off to get Rayna and shown her.

It was the Brotherhood of the Egg, or people a lot like them. They were dressed in the same ridiculous costumes, though they all seemed older. There was a big church just down the road that they seemed to be using as a base, because every so often groups of them would come out of it, like bees from a hive, and buzz off in several different directions.

"Why are they doing this?" I'd asked Rayna. "I thought the chickens were just ignoring them, but they seem to be working together here. Why?"

She'd turned to me with eyes shining. "There must not be enough chickens to keep the area secure. They must need humans to help them watch."

"Why are you saying that like it's a good thing?"

"Because that means there may be a way we can get in."

It was a lot more dangerous in daylight. When we finally did sneak out, we weren't able to get far. When we were almost at the perimeter we had to duck into a house when we heard people coming. We were stuck there for the rest of the day but that did have an unexpected benefit. The people *were* a huge bunch of the Brotherhood, marching with another batch of chicken commandos to a park just across the road. And there they ran drills.

I've seen many weird and funny things since the chickens came, but these drills were something else.

The Brotherhood tried marching around the grass, but they weren't organised and kept getting in each other's way. I was trying so hard not to laugh by the third time that two of the Brotherhood walked into each other that Rayna sent me to another room so that I wouldn't give us away. I got back just in time to see the Commandos take a turn. If anything, they were worse. They just spent all their time rushing from one side of the field to the other. One of them had to be new, judging by his size and clumsiness. He kept tripping over his own feet and falling into the others. Their leader, who had an impressively large comb, kept stalking over and squawking at him. Finally he was sent off to stand with the Brotherhood. By this point I had to go back to the other room until I'd calmed down. I took the notes with me and started trying to find a way around their defences. They looked shambolic – but that didn't mean they'd be easy to defeat.

Night began to fall and I pored over the notes as the streetlights started coming on outside. After twenty minutes of counting everything up I sat back on my heels and shook my head.

"Rayna, this isn't going to work. Rayna?"

There was no sign of her. I got up and walked into the next room, but she wasn't there either. I began to get frantic. I dashed through every room in the house, calling her name as loudly as I dared. But she wasn't there. Rayna had gone.

I sat down on a bed in one of the upstairs rooms.

What was I going to do? I couldn't think of any reason Rayna could have for leaving the house. Had she been taken? Should I get out while I could?

I was agonising over it, frozen to the bed in shock. Then I heard the back door slowly creak open and softly snap shut. Then footsteps on the stairs, coming closer.

"Jesse?" At first I didn't recognise the voice, but as it came a second time I knew it was Rayna.

"In here," I called back. The door opened and her head poked round. She was grinning.

I scowled back. "Where were you?" I asked. "I was worried to death. I thought you'd been taken."

She shrugged. "I went to have a look at the perimeter. I wanted to see how big an area the chickens are protecting."

"Huh." I gathered up the notes and began packing everything into my backpack. "And?"

She began to grin again. "It's too big for them to control properly. To keep the mast safe they've got to patrol a massive area. They've got to walk almost a mile around it. And the Brotherhood headquarters aren't even inside that area!"

I settled the backpack on securely. "That doesn't matter, Rayna. We still don't have a chance."

Her grin slipped away. "What?"

I gestured out the window. "I counted up everyone they've got here. There's about five Catchers, at least two squads of Commandos and who knows how many of the Brotherhood there are. There's a Commando squad by the generator at all times and we couldn't slip past them. We'd have to fight – and as soon as we do, everyone will know that we're there and all of the chickens around here come and get us. Maybe all the Catchers in Aberdeen. It can't be done."

"Huh," Rayna said thoughtfully. "So what we need is a distraction."

"What we need," I said levelly, "is an army."

She nodded. "I might know where to get one."

CHAPTER 11

We set out right after that, clambering over the same wall as the night before as soon as the Catcher on patrol had rounded the corner. The dark still felt as spooky as it had the night before, but something was different. I think it was Rayna. She was striding along, barely looking from left to right, confidence radiating off her. Nothing was going to get in her way.

Rayna led us up a street called Clifton Road and into a house about halfway up. It seemed that she had another base hidden away here. I wondered exactly how many she had scattered all over the place.

I certainly couldn't fault her on her choice. The flat was up on the second floor. And even though it was late, I could see enough of the garden to see that it bordered all the other gardens belonging to the houses on the block. In other words, if anyone came for us we'd have a good getaway route. The flat was high enough up that we'd be able to see any trouble from a mile away. We'd already had tea so there was nothing left to do but go to sleep. We both slept in separate rooms that night, on beds. And unlike the night before I could actually appreciate them, feeling safe and snug.

I woke in the morning with a ray of sunshine gently tickling my eyelids. I groaned and rolled over. I felt a lot better than I had yesterday. My arms and legs didn't hurt as much from being tied up. I guess a day of walking had stretched out my muscles nicely. I got to my feet and headed out to find Rayna.

She was on the top floor of the two that the house had, staring out of a bedroom window at a view. It was pretty glorious, showing the sparkling blue sea and stretching to the horizon. The University Library building rose out of the city as if it had been purposely built to block out part of the sea. From here it looked even less natural, alien from its surroundings.

"I can see why you hate that building so much," I said by way of greeting. Rayna stayed where she was, looking out unblinkingly like a cat.

"Mmm," was all she said.

I squinted at the library. "If it's over there then we could have just spent the night there. Did we have to stay here?"

"Oh we had to, all right. It was the safest thing to do."

I noticed that she wasn't looking at the sea, but was focused on one thing in particular. I followed the direction of her gaze and realised she was looking at a squat building just across the road from us. As

I watched, I thought I saw movement in one of the windows.

"Is that where we're going to find our army?" I asked. She nodded, still staring at it.

"I hope so. But this isn't the sort of place where you want to get caught unawares. If we're going there then we need to be careful. They don't take kindly to people being smart with them. And you can't try and threaten them like you did with Glen. In fact, it's probably better that you don't speak at all."

"But they like you?"

Finally she dragged herself away from the window. "Like is too strong a word. They put up with me from time to time because they know I've got useful connections. They're tough and they don't take any nonsense."

"So they're exactly what we want?"

"Yup." She stretched and headed for the stairs. "If we survive the experience."

From a distance, even if it was only from a street away, the building hadn't looked that big. From the ground looking up at it was a completely different story. It seemed to tower above me, threatening to do me harm.

A battered sign read 'Kittybrewster Primary School'. It looked more like a prison. There was a fence and a wall all around it. The building itself sat in the middle of a concrete playground. The original building, Victorian like the rest of the area, had probably been a square, but an extension had been added on the side, huddling close to the older building like a small child seeking protection. There were large windows on the top two floors. You got the feeling that if this had been a prison then no one would have escaped. Nothing could cross the playground without being seen. Which I suppose made it an excellent stronghold. Though it also meant that we'd probably be spotted as soon as we made a move.

If we hadn't been spotted already.

We were barely in the gate before the door opened before us. I couldn't see anyone there. I gulped, but Rayna didn't even hesitate, just marched forward into the black opening. I followed. It felt like I was walking into the waiting maw of some great beast.

I found myself in what looked like a small waiting area. There were chairs scattered around and most of them were occupied with kids, all looking quite tough, who just sat and watched us as we went past. Rayna didn't seem to see them. She just walked straight ahead and into a second door. I went after her, though I could feel the watching eyes on my back.

Again, I was reminded of a prison. It was one huge space inside, rising up, with walkways on each level. And they were filled with people. There must have been close on a hundred of them, all staring down at us, not making a sound.

On our level there were only a handful of guys. Rayna walked straight up to one and stopped in front of him.

"Percy," she said to him.

It was a close competition, but he had to be the biggest, nastiest guy in there. In a normal world I'm pretty sure that he'd have been in prison by now.

"Ambassador," he said in a voice like a bloodhound's growl. I could almost imagine his mouth being full of fangs. I stopped a little way behind Rayna and tried to look like I was watching her back. "What brings you here?"

"You do," she said without flinching. "I want you and your guys."

"Ooooh," he said mocking her. The call was taken up by everyone around him until the air faintly hummed with jeers and tension. "And what do you want us for?"

"A job."

"And what would that be?"

"To take down the chickens."

I have no idea how Rayna could ever have thought that I was braver than her. She just stood there, staring down this great thug. I would have cut and run about half a minute ago, right when he had started talking. Actually, I wouldn't have gone in here in the first place.

Percy just laughed at her. "And what if I said no?"

"Don't be stupid," she said to him evenly. "You know that isn't your decision to make. Get your boss and I'll talk to him."

This guy wasn't even in charge? I actually shivered slightly to think of what Percy's boss would be like.

Percy was scratching his head. "Well I don't know. He's asleep about now and it wouldn't be right to wake him up for some weak little girl..."

His voice trailed off suggestively and Rayna's eyes narrowed. I felt that she knew exactly what he wanted. "So that's what it's going to take, is it?" she asked.

"Yeah, I guess it is," he replied.

Rayna glanced around quickly as if looking for some other way out of her situation, then shrugged and backed away.

"Jesse, hand me that chair there," She called back over her shoulder, never breaking eye contact with Percy.

I looked around and found a plastic chair lying just beside me, just the right size for someone like me to sit on. I picked it up and carried it over to her, placing it into her outstretched hand. "What are you doing?" I whispered to her.

"What must be done. Now back off."

I did, quickly. Across from her I could see someone doing the same for Percy. I realised what was going on a second before he gave a cry and sprang at her, swinging wildly.

I had never seen gladiator combat with chairs before, but within a second I realised that it wasn't as stupid as it sounded. There was a fair amount of strategy to it that wouldn't have occurred to me. For one thing, the point didn't seem to be to hit the other person. Both were trying to knock the other's chair away.

Rayna had caught Percy's first charge with the legs of her chair and they were locked in place, legs entangled with legs, like stags with their horns caught. Then with a shrug of her shoulders she twisted to the side and he went rolling off, landing hard on the floor.

He didn't let go of his chair, though. He kept a tight grasp of it. He scrambled back to his feet and walked forward again, more carefully this time, calculating. This time it was Rayna who darted in, thrusting her chair forward. He caught it with his and lifted them both up and away, but she had been ready for it and moved forward, twisting as she did so. He had to let go of the chair with one hand or else lose it completely – and that was when she struck.

She moved in a tight circle, putting her chair firmly down on the ground then hopping up on it and jumping at him. Percy was already off balance and he fell backwards, hitting the floor with a solid thud. It must have stunned him, because he didn't react fast enough to stop Rayna grabbing her own chair and bringing it down on top of him.

There was a hush as everyone stared down at what had just happened. Percy lay on the ground, the four legs of the chair surrounding him like a cage, trapping his clothes to the ground. And on top of the chair sat

Rayna, panting slightly. She stuck out her tongue at him and said, "I win."

I began clapping. I felt that someone should or else they might start throwing things. There was a tense moment or two then others joined in and finally they were all at it, cheering for the hero and booing the fallen warrior.

It drove Percy mad. With a great heave, he managed to rock the chair enough to get free and surged to his feet. Rayna fell backwards, a shocked look on her face. She tried to get up, but before she could Percy was upon her. He lifted her chair and was about to bring it down when a sharp, clear voice rang out.

"Stop."

Percy froze and looked around guiltily, focusing on a point a little past my left ear. If he was acting like that then the owner of the voice could only be his boss. And that person was standing right behind me.

I turned around slowly, trying to not gulp. And there stood the guy in charge of this murderous bunch.

Frankly, I expected someone taller.

He was bigger than me, but only just. I only had to stand on tiptoes and I would be able to look him in the eye. He wasn't muscly like Percy, either. He was slender and held himself well. For a moment I wasn't sure I was looking at the right person.

But every eye in the place was on him and he had their complete attention. He paced past me and I moved out of his way, not wanting to catch his anger.

There was an aura about him of someone who was perfectly in control of himself and his surroundings.

He walked over to Percy, who was trying to be as still as possible. The chair was wobbling where he held it over his head, his arms obviously getting tired.

"The Ambassador won, Percy." His voice was like ice; cold, sharp and precise. I couldn't see his expression, but Percy could. He looked scared.

"You cheated."

"Yes, sir." Percy's voice came out small. I was surprised that he could speak in anything less than a roar. "I'm sorry, sir."

"Yes."

Then, in a quick movement, the leader of over one hundred violent kids grabbed Percy and threw him to the ground.

It happened almost too fast to be seen. Percy slammed into the floor and the chair clattered down next to him. He lay still and for a second I was worried that he'd been hurt, but then he raised his head slightly and I realised that he just didn't want his leader to take any more notice of him.

Rayna had looked shocked for an instant, but then carefully smoothed her features into a mask, giving nothing away.

"Cody," she said, in greeting.

"Ambassador," he replied, bowing his head slightly. "And I see that you've brought a friend. Shall we talk in my office?"

His office turned out to be on the first floor and I was pretty sure it had belonged to the headmaster back when this had been a school. It was neat and tidy, everything put in place almost obsessively. Cody sat behind a desk without paper, though a useless computer still sat there. We sat on the other side, in chairs that were slightly lower down. I'm pretty sure he'd done that on purpose.

"Well, well, well," he said, looking at us. "I didn't expect you to get a partner, Ambassador. You look ready to be married."

"We're just working together," she quickly replied, though I noticed that she'd blushed slightly. Cody nodded in agreement.

"Yes, quite. By the way, I should apologise for Percy's behaviour back there. Though you put on an excellent show. I was watching from up here." He tilted his head to one side. "So, why are you here?"

Rayna leaned forward, making sure to keep eye contact. "I need your guys, this little army you've built up."

"Oh? And what for? Has some group been causing trouble?"

Rayna shook her head, very deliberately. "No. I need you to help me take down the chickens."

He was very interested in that, though he tried to hide it. But I was watching him closely and saw his eyes widen a fraction. "Then you're being stupid. There's nothing we can do to hurt them. We wouldn't stand a chance."

"Come on, Cody. You know who I am and what I've been trying to do. Do you think that I'd come here and ask if I wasn't positive?" In quick, clean sentences she explained what we had learned.

Cody was leaning back in his chair. "Say that I do believe you. I've got a good set-up here. Why should I change that? What do I get out of it?"

Rayna was quiet for a moment and so I answered for her.

"We can get you food and clothes," I told him. After all, that was why I was here. To offer the resources of my group.

He turned his gaze to me and smiled thinly. "I don't need any, thanks. I've got enough."

I frowned. "You must have more than a hundred guys out there. How can you have enough?"

"Simple," he replied. "Because I'm not stupid."

"In the first few days after the chicken attack Cody took control of this group," Rayna said at my side. "It was smaller then, but he knew that he'd need a lot of things for them to survive. So he marched them right down the road and to the Sainsbury's there. He left a force there to protect it against anyone else and brought the rest of his group back here with everything they could carry. Occasionally they have to make another supply run but it's going to be there for a fair while. He's got a pretty good grip on rationing."

Cody kept smiling at me. "Offer me something else if you like, but I don't see that there's much point. After all, there's nothing I could want."

"How about just for the good of mankind? You'd be helping a lot of people."

He just laughed. "Oh, I do like jokes." He leaned forward, his expression unpleasant. "Tell me another."

I opened my mouth, about to do exactly what he wanted but Rayna kicked my foot before I could. I looked at her but her head was bowed forward and her face was twisted in thought.

"Fine," she said at last. "What do you want?"

Cody tilted his head slightly, as if he found this fascinating. "What do I want?" he repeated. He leaned forward. "There's a Catcher patrolling around my Outer Defences. I want you to take it out."

There was stunned silence. "You want us to take down a Catcher?" I said at last. There was no way we could take down one of those. Not without a huge army.

He smiled smugly at me. "Well, you claim to have found some great weakness of theirs. This gives you a chance to prove it."

"It wasn't our plan to actually fight the chickens. We'd just cause a distraction and then take down the mast." I glanced sideways at Rayna. She was leaning her chin on her hands, deep in thought.

Cody shook his head. "No. Your plan was for me and my guys to cause the distraction. We're the ones at risk. So before we do this we need to know that it'll actually work. And for that you need to take down that Catcher."

"But that's insane..." I began before Rayna interrupted.

"Quiet, Jesse. You've got yourself a deal, Cody."

I stared at her while Cody grinned.

"Excellent," he said, holding out a hand. Rayna glared at it for a moment then grabbed it and shook.

"We'll need some supplies and some of your people though," she told him. He nodded.

"Tell Percy what you need and he'll set it up." Cody leaned back in his chair. "You can go now."

I didn't like being dismissed like that and I could tell that Rayna didn't either, but she got up and left. Once we were outside the door I grabbed her arm.

"Rayna, are you crazy? We can't take on one of those things."

She shook me off but wouldn't meet my eyes. "Don't worry," she said. "I've got a plan."

CHAPTER 12

The day dawned bright and sunny and that got on my nerves. The day had no right to be sunny. By the time night came we could all have been eaten by this Catcher. There should have been brooding clouds and thunder rumbling in the distance. Not sun and a cool spring breeze.

Sleeping at Kittybrewster was odd enough. The place was packed full of kids, mostly boys, though there were a few tough looking girls in there as well. In Noah's gang we usually had a sleeping compartment to ourselves or else we had to share with maybe one other person. In here everyone was packed into classrooms sharing mattresses on the floor.

Cody didn't even offer us breakfast. While everyone else tucked into tins, Rayna and I had to have more cereal bars from our backpack. I guess that Cody thought that he'd done enough for us, letting us stay the night and use some of his people, but I was running dangerously low on supplies. We'd already run out of tinned food and I was saving my chocolate bars for an emergency.

After breakfast he handed us some rolls of tin foil that he'd found in the school kitchen and introduced us to the people we'd be working with. A tall, thin guy called Billy was our runner. There were two bulky guys who looked vaguely like brothers. None of them seemed that friendly. Rayna took one look at them and shrugged.

"OK, you'll do," she said.

We also got a guide, a small, nervous boy called Paul. I wasn't sure what he was doing with a bunch of guys like this, but it turned out that he was an excellent scout and Cody treated him well because of that. He was partly in charge of the 'Outer Defences,' – a scattering of kids patrolling the surrounding area. They kept an eye out for chickens, other kids and anything else that might cause problems.

"There's been a Catcher snooping around up here for the past week or so," Paul said as he led the way. "It's been around about the Hilton area."

Rayna looked impressed and slightly concerned. "You have guys that far away?"

"We have guys all over."

We walked up the side road on to Clifton Road, where we'd slept the night before last, and turned right. Where the road ended, we scrabbled up a footpath on to another road. More houses. These ones were different though. Where a front door should be there was just a gaping, cave-like opening, with some stairs leading up and away. I guess there were flats up there. It looked kind of weird.

"You set up," Paul said, glancing around. "I'll go find out where that Catcher got to."

Rayna uncoiled the rope from where she'd been carrying it around her shoulders and threw one end to one of the brothers. "OK, listen up," she said. "We know there's a Catcher in the area. What we've got to do is to take it down. Paul's gone to find it. Then we'll have Billy lure it over here."

"How am I supposed to do that?" Billy asked.

"Jump around in front of it, throw rocks at it, whatever. Just get it to chase you. Then you lead it over here. We'll lay the rope across the road and pull it up just in time to trip the chicken up."

"What then?" The other brother asked. I could see the three of them exchanging glances. They obviously didn't think that this was a good idea. I couldn't help but agree, though I didn't say it.

"We've got information that leads us to believe that the chickens are controlled by signals. If we can block out that signal then the chicken should just shut down. So the second it hits the dust we wrap it in tin foil."

"Like a Christmas turkey?" I asked.

She sighed, but nodded. "Like a Christmas turkey. Try and focus on its head. I think that's the most likely place for the receiver to be."

Paul silently appeared at that moment and muttered something to Rayna. She motioned the others into position. Billy went off with Paul, and the other two went across the road holding the rope. Rayna glanced around and then wrapped her end once around a lamppost, to give it extra strength.

"Rayna, are you sure about this?" I muttered to her. She glared at me.

"Of course I am. It's foolproof. We just trip it and wrap it."

I looked at the rolls of tin foil that Cody had got for us. They didn't seem very strong. At that moment Glen's theory seemed even weaker.

"So it'll be like that bit from Star Wars, with the Ewoks and the chicken walker?"

She rolled her eyes and nodded. "Yes, like that."

I was about to say something else when the ground began to shake. "Get ready," Rayna called. She picked up her end of the rope. "Give me a hand with this."

I grabbed it just as Billy came haring around the corner, the chicken not far behind him. He was running flat out. I don't think I've ever seen anyone run faster. But the chicken was gaining.

Billy flashed across the rope, his arms raised like it was the finishing line.

"Pull!" roared Rayna. She heaved the rope up and wrapped it around the post a few more times, the group on the other side doing the same. We all pulled it taut just as the chicken reached it. I think it saw the rope a second before it hit it because it began to slow down. It didn't make any difference though. The chicken smashed into the rope...

...and kept on going.

The post beside us was wrenched from the ground and we were pulled from our feet. I dimly saw the same happening to the other group, the railing they'd tied their rope to clattering along the ground. We were dragged along as the chicken took another step.

"That's what happened in Star Wars as well," I muttered when we finally stopped moving. While Rayna only groaned beside me I looked up, desperate to see what had happened to the chicken.

Billy had slowed down after passing the rope, chest heaving. He turned round, thinking that the plan had worked, a grin on his face, just as the chicken reached him. His grin just had time to fade before the chicken pecked him up, its metal beak clacking shut. It tilted its head back and I could almost hear poor Billy slithering down its throat.

Then the Catcher turned round.

"Rayna," I said urgently. "Come on, get up. We've got to go."

I scrambled to my feet, Rayna not far behind. The chicken took a step towards us. The other team had fled and the chicken had no one to focus on but us.

I grabbed Rayna, who was still a bit groggy, and pulled her along with me. She shook her head and then began to run faster. We weren't as fast as Billy had been and if we carried on along the road we'd get eaten for sure. So we swerved through the hedge beside us and pounded up the path. Lasers from the chicken's eyes flashed past us and hit the wall of the house, charring it slightly. The mouth of the house loomed in front of us, gaping and hungry. We plunged in, dashing up the stairs into the darkness. Hiding up there we panted, catching our breath and wondering if we'd escaped.

There was a squawk and the chicken thrust its head up after us. We screamed and ran up further, the chicken snapping its beak at us. In a flurry we rattled the door handles and managed to get through the one on the right. We scuttled through and ran through to the back. I was in such a rush that I tripped and fell, grabbing Rayna and pulling her down with me. It was only after we started sliding that I realised the chicken was pushing the house over, desperate to get us.

It wanted revenge.

We landed on the far wall with a thump and rolled to our feet. The window was right in front of us, getting closer to the ground with every passing second. The handles were stiff, but in the end we managed to fumble them open and then we were through, spilling out of the window and on to the grass not so far below. There was a sharp crack behind us and we dashed forward as the whole house collapsed.

We turned and looked back, coughing in the dust that was billowing all around us. All that could be seen of the chicken was its head, poking out of a mound of bricks and rubble. It screeched and thrashed and the bricks began to tumble away.

"Quick, Jesse, the tinfoil."

I was on to my feet in a shot and back round the side of the house. The tin foil was where we'd left it, still sitting by the side of the road. I grabbed it up and turned. Rayna had climbed up beside the chicken and I tossed the packet like a javelin. It landed beside her and she pounced upon it, tearing it open and frantically wrapping it again and again round the metal head beside her. I got one look at the chicken's mad eye, gleaming at me evilly, before the silvery sheet hid it from view.

It didn't go quietly. It thrashed from side to side, firing its eye lasers. They burned through the tin foil and only just missed hitting Rayna. The rest of the foil glowed and sparked, making the chicken squawk in pain. It must have done more damage to itself, because she quickly replaced the foil and it didn't try again. Finally, it was still. Rayna didn't stop wrapping until all the foil was used up. Then she slowly sat back.

Peace descended. I could hear birds chirping in the trees and a banging from inside the chicken that must have been Billy trying to fight his way out. But from the chicken there was nothing. Not a creak. Not a crow. It was completely still.

"You've done it."

Rayna didn't respond at first, just stood there looking down at it, a confused look on her face. "Yeah, I guess I have."

After a moment she slowly pulled back her leg and

kicked the chicken's head. Her foot bounced off the side with a clang. She did it again, with more force this time. Then she started jumping up and down, yelling and screaming at the top of her voice.

"Yes! Yes! We did it! We finally did it. We took one of them down! Cody can't say no after this!"

CHAPTER 13

"No."

Rayna just stared at Cody for a second, trying to process this. "What did you just say?" she hissed.

He looked back at her, his face like stone. "I said no."

I sat in the too-small chair, staring dully in front of me. It had already been a long day and it was barely lunchtime yet. Before anything else we'd had to dig the Catcher out so that we could get Billy back. It was nerve-wracking – with every movement we were worried that it would get the signal back. Finally, we managed to shift enough rubble to be able to prise open the hatch in its stomach. He came out swaggering, boasting about how no chicken could contain him, but after we'd gathered up the other three and started back he got more and more quiet. I guess the shock of what had just happened must have hit him after the adrenaline wore off.

We'd arrived back as heroes. People were chanting our names as we entered the school and even Percy looked a bit impressed. The noise drew Cody out of his office and he shut it up with a quick command. Then we came into his office, expecting to be offered his help.

Instead we got this.

"Why?" Rayna looked completely confused at this. I felt the same. Why wouldn't he want to see the chickens defeated?

"It's simple. The chickens aren't a threat to us."

"They clearly are," I said, before common sense told me to shut up. Cody just looked at me.

"They don't know where we are and they've shown no real interest in tracking us down. I don't think they even really care about us. If the odd one comes after us then we've got the means to take them down. I don't see what use all-out war would be. We aren't guaranteed victory and thanks to your plan there's a good chance we'd lose. I'm not willing to take that risk."

"The chickens will come for you one day. They won't just let us be." Rayna thumped a fist down onto Cody's desk. He didn't seem impressed.

"Yes, so you say. So you've been saying for months. But it's not happened yet. We're still here and I don't think antagonising the chickens is going to solve anything."

"What was taking down that Catcher if not antagonising the chickens?" I asked. He looked at me and raised an eyebrow.

"That was self-defence. It threatened us. If we didn't deal with it then it could have exposed us. And now it's not a problem any more. Why change that?"

"Cody, you rat! You promised! You... what is it?" Rayna stopped mid-rant to snap at Percy as he came in.

"Cody, we've caught some people approaching the building. A guy and a small girl."

"So?" Cody asked, looking at his lieutenant.

"They say they're here to talk to the Ambassador."

I looked at Rayna and mouthed "Glen and Lizzie?" She shrugged.

"Bring them up," she told Percy. He looked to Cody and waited for his nod before disappearing. He returned a moment later with Glen and Lizzie. Lizzie was looking kind of white and she ran to give me a hug as soon as she saw me. I couldn't help feeling a bit touched that she cared so much.

Glen froze when he saw Cody. He swallowed and turned to talk to Rayna directly. "Ambassador, you've got to see this."

"Oh?" she asked. "What is it?"

"It popped up on the TV channels a couple of hours ago." He pulled his coat back to reveal his portable TV under one arm. He must have got it working while we were away.

Glen moved forward to put it on the desk, then hesitated and looked at Cody for permission. He nodded and Glen put down his burden, fiddling with it a bit while everyone else gathered in front. Cody came out from behind the desk, leaning forward slightly so he had a good view. But when the machine was turned on all that filled the screen was static.

"It's been on repeat. Hang on."

The static flickered and then an image popped on to the screen. It was a chicken.

I stared at it. This wasn't one of the gigantic robot chickens. It wasn't even one of the Commandos we'd seen marching about at Beechgrove. It was just a normal chicken. Wearing a hat.

It wasn't a normal hat. It looked like someone had taken a colander or a big lampshade and covered it in tinfoil. It was twice the size of the chicken's head and was attached with a headband or something. It looked like it was in some sort of command centre or a lab. There were monitors on the walls behind it and lots of computers and stuff in the background. Even after everything I'd seen over the last few months it was bizarre.

And then it spoke.

"Children of the humans," it said. At least I assume it was the chicken speaking. Its mouth didn't move. The voice just echoed around the room while it stared into the camera. "I am your new leader. I know that some of you are still out there and some might even have ideas about fighting back. That is futile. For too long our race has been enslaved by yours. Now is our time. Now we will break free and take back the world."

The TV cut away from the chicken. It showed Edinburgh and then London. Giant Catchers were striding about the streets in front of Edinburgh Castle and the Houses of Parliament, obviously in complete control. The voice spoke over this.

"Your government has fallen. Your police force is scattered. We were created by your army and now your army is ours. The United Kingdom is ours. And this is only the beginning."

More shots. Giant chickens fighting with soldiers in front of the Eiffel Tower. A robot chicken standing by the White House. A rooster crowing over a pyramid.

"You have no chance against us. We will win. So join us now."

Another shot. It was somewhere in the country, showing big fields of corn. People were working, planting and tending the fields. I felt a shiver run through me. I guess now we knew what had happened to the adults. They were being used like slaves.

"You will be safe. You will be cared for."

Then the chicken came back. Its eyes looked insane. It spoke for the final time. "But if you stand against us we will find you. And we will take you."

Then the screen went black.

There was silence for a moment. Then Rayna spat on the ground. "So we're doing this now, right?"

"Definitely," Cody said, his eyes still on the screen. The silence stretched out, then he blinked and the moment was broken.

"I guess there's no point in having an army if you're not going to do anything with it," he said, straightening up. He looked at Rayna and me, pinning us in place with his gaze. "We're not doing this alone. You two are coming along with us. And that group you represent."

"Umm... I don't really have the authority to decide that..." I began, but Rayna cut me off.

"They'll be there. Their leader said that he was in. He will stand with us."

Cody looked between the two of us, his eyebrow raised. "Forgive me if I don't just take your word for it. I'd rather know for sure that your leader will be there. It'll take a while to get organised here. Why don't you go and ask him yourself?"

Rayna nodded and both she and Cody stood up at the same time. He reached into a desk drawer and pulled out a piece of paper. He scribbled something on it then handed it to her.

"Here," he said. "You can move freely throughout my territory. Make sure you hurry back now."

Rayna took it and clenched it tightly in a fist before shoving it into her pocket. "Come on, Jesse," she said, grabbing my arm. I made sure that Lizzie was still with me and together we left the office, while Cody stood behind us, still deep in thought.

CHAPTER 14

"He's pretty scary," I said to Rayna as we headed back to the train station. Ever since the meeting with Cody had ended she'd been in a foul humour, stomping along and kicking whatever lay in her way. Even Lizzie knew that something was wrong and was walking along quietly instead of running and yelling like she usually did. Glen had headed back to his library as soon as he could.

"He's a jerk. But he's a useful one," she said through clenched teeth. "I never like being around him, but I can't deny that he runs things well."

Cody's 'territory' apparently extended for quite a distance in every direction. Rayna was able to take us a much quicker route, back along Clifton Road and by the Sainsbury's that kept him and his army fed. As we were walking past a guard appeared on the road before us, vaulting over a fence from where he'd been hiding in some bushes, and demanding identification. I could almost hear Rayna's teeth gritting, but she pulled out the paper that Cody had given her and showed it to the guard. He looked it over and nodded.

"That's fine, thank you, Ambassador. You'd best be careful if you're going in that direction though. There have been reports of a Catcher down that way."

Rayna nodded, her expression still grim, and took the bit of paper back from the guard. She kept walking without saying anything. I hurried after her with Lizzie in my wake. I was instantly worried. There might have been shops around here but there was a whole car park between us and them. If there really was a chicken somewhere around here then there wouldn't be much chance to hide.

Rayna didn't seem to care about that and just kept marching on, her expression thoughtful. We were about halfway along the road before she finally said what was on her mind.

"Do you agree with him?" she asked me.

I was too busy keeping an eye out for the chicken to remember what we had been talking about so I just raised my eyes at her. "With who?" I asked.

"With Cody. What do you think of the plan?"

I thought I heard something in the distance and froze, trying to see if it came again, but after a minute of listening I couldn't hear anything. "It does seem like a pretty big risk. He's got a lot of guys behind him, but the chickens were able to capture most of the adults in Aberdeen in a just a few days. Noah's guys are well organised, but if we don't even have any weapons that can take them on then what are we supposed to do?"

"Do you think we need more people?" she asked.

I thought about it for a second. "Well it probably couldn't hurt," I replied. "Do you think you could get some?"

She nodded. "Yeah, there's a few groups that I think would be up for it. I'm just not sure that we could get them all together in time."

I was about to agree with her, but then the ground wobbled slightly beneath me. I froze, as did Rayna. We looked at each other for a moment in panic.

Usually if there was a chicken coming I could feel the vibrations long before they were noticeable. But I hadn't been paying proper attention, too busy thinking about the battle ahead. And in that time the chicken had somehow been able to sneak up on us.

I looked around frantically. Thankfully we'd passed the large car park behind and were now stuck in the middle of a crossroads. I couldn't see the chicken anywhere and that hopefully meant that it couldn't see me. There was an old church nearby. Both Rayna and I ran towards it at the same time. I grabbed Lizzie as we went past and dragged her along with me. We made it to the door and slipped inside. We carefully closed the door behind us, making sure that we didn't make a noise and attract attention. Then we lay flat on the floor.

"Ouch, let go," Lizzie squealed, tugging her arm away from me. "You're hurting me."

I released her but clapped a hand over her mouth instead. "Lizzie, you've got to be very quiet," I told her.

She squirmed a bit and I took my hand away, putting one finger to my lips and going "Shhhh."

She repeated the gesture and nodded. Then said, in a whisper, "Why?"

"Because there's a giant chicken out there," Rayna hissed at her. "And we're hiding from it."

"Why are you hiding from the chickens?" she asked. "They only want to help us."

Rayna and I exchanged a look. We'd been hoping that she would have forgotten everything that the cult had told her by now. I guess, thinking about it, that it was a bit naïve.

"No they're not," I told her very calmly. "They want to grab you and take you far away. That's why you have to be quiet."

She shook her head firmly. "No, the chickens are good to us. And you said that you believed that too. Back at the church."

"I was lying," I told her. "I'll explain it later but for now you've got to trust me."

"Lies are evil," she whispered, but settled down and didn't say anything else. I let out a breath, relieved.

The ground shook once again and a bulk blocked out the light from one of the windows. A shadow sprayed itself across the floor. It was the shadow of a gigantic fowl.

We'd got Lizzie to be quiet just in time. The chicken was here.

It stood outside for what felt like hours, occasionally

turning its head from side to side as if looking for something. Finally, though, there was a reassuring thud as it took one of its huge steps and moved away.

Rayna let out a gasp of air beside me. "It took its time," she said, her voice still pitched low.

"Well you know how dedicated they are," I replied. "They work eggs-tra hard."

She rolled her eyes at me and didn't reply. Lizzie laughed a bit but it sounded forced. I looked down at her and found her staring back with large worried eyes.

"What's wrong?" I asked her.

"Chickens aren't bad," she told me seriously. "They're the good guys."

"I'll explain it to you later, OK? For now you've just got to trust me."

"OK," she said, though she didn't sound very sure. I turned around and saw Rayna already leaving the church. I walked after her but by the time I stepped outside she was already a fair distance down the road. The wrong road.

"Rayna, where are you going?" I called after her softly. There was still a giant chicken around.

"You're right, Jesse. We need more people. So you go talk to Noah and I'm going to go round some up."

"Where will we meet up?" I hoped I didn't sound desperate, but I had a bad feeling about this.

"I'll see you back at the train station a little later, OK? If Noah agrees with the plan, tell him to get everyone to the Aberdeen Market in two days' time. Make sure you go in through the side entrance, not the one on Union Street. Everyone else will be there then. OK?"

"OK," I called after her as she turned away. "Walk softly." I had no idea what that meant but I'd seen it in a movie once and it sounded cool.

She smiled at me. "You too," she said. Then she turned her back and was gone.

We got to the station and, just like a few days ago, Noah was there waiting for us, sitting on the edge of one of the platforms and dangling his feet in the air. I guess the lookouts must have told him that we were coming. Not much got past Noah.

"Jesse," he greeted me. Then he looked at Lizzie and raised his eyebrows. "And is that the Ambassador? Did you shrink her or something?"

Lizzie giggled and shook her head. "My name is Lizzie." She held out her hand, as a proud parent had probably taught her to do a while ago.

Noah's eyebrows rose even further and he jumped down onto the tracks, taking the outstretched hand and shaking it solemnly. "Where did you find this one, Jesse? There must be quite a story behind it."

"You have no idea," I told him. "We've got a lot to talk about. We should probably do it soon."

He nodded to me, then bent down and swept Lizzie up into the air. He was stronger than he looked.

He put her on his back then turned to me and nodded. "All right, let's go."

We walked along the track together and I was surprised at how nice it felt. I wouldn't have believed it a few days ago, but I'd missed this place in the time that I'd been away. I guess it was a kind of home. I didn't like it while I was there, but a little time away had made me appreciate it more.

We got on the train and Noah sent Lizzie off to play. She had an odd look on her face but nodded in agreement and scampered off. Then he led me into his office.

I sat on one of the beds while he sat on another and I told him about everything that had happened, leaving out very little. The only thing I left out was the Brotherhood of the Egg. Rayna had known about it for months and she hadn't told him. She had to have a good reason. And if he found that she'd been keeping important information like that of him then he might decide to pull out from the attack. So instead I just told him that we'd picked Lizzie up while looking for the TV. Noah nodded along and asked a few good questions from time to time so that he could get a better idea of what was going on. Eventually I was finished and he was quiet for a long while, mulling things over.

"Well, that's quite a tale," he said at last. "So now we've got to back up this Cody guy or it was all basically worthless?"

I nodded. "Basically. Rayna is right. This is a golden opportunity. And it could be the only one we've got."

Noah shook his head and ran a hand over his forehead. "Is that really what you think? Truly?"

I shrugged. "I don't think we've much of a choice. Either it happens now or it never happens at all. We will never be more ready for this. I really don't like it, I'll be honest with you. But that's the way things are."

Noah nodded abruptly and straightened up. "Good job," he said, patting me on the shoulder. "I knew I'd made a good decision in choosing you to go with her."

"I thought that you only sent me out because you found me annoying."

I'd meant to say it jokingly but it came out a lot more seriously than I was expecting it to. I hadn't expected saying it aloud to hurt quite that much.

Noah looked down at me and shook his head. "Do you really think that?"

I nodded, unable to meet his eyes. I heard him sigh.

"So you thought that I sent you out on all those missions, more than anyone else, because...?"

"Because no one would really care if I got caught." I finished his sentence, though I didn't really want to. A second later I felt his hand pat me on the shoulder and looked up to see him crouched down before me.

"You're an idiot," he said, though he said it with feeling. "I sent you out so often because you're good at it. You're a smart guy and I knew that any group you went with would have a better chance of succeeding. I thought you knew that too. I didn't know that you felt like this."

I frowned. "But if that was the case then why didn't you put me in charge? It was always someone else leading. I could have done it."

"I think you know the answer to that," he told me gently.

I nodded. I did.

"They don't really respect me," I said.

"Because....?"

"Because of the chicken jokes."

"Because of the chicken jokes." He echoed. "I understand that you can laugh at our enemies but you've got to know that others don't. They just think that you're being dumb. They wouldn't follow someone who didn't take things seriously. Maybe there will be a time when we can laugh about it, but right now we're all too scared. You've got to know that."

I did know. I guess I had always known. But this was the first time I'd cared.

I suddenly felt exhausted. The last few days had really taken a toll on me. I yawned and Noah noticed.

"Get some sleep," he ordered. "I'll tell you when the Ambassador is back."

I tried to get up but couldn't quite manage it. He rolled his eyes and pushed me back on to his bed. I was just able to get my shoes off so that I didn't make his covers filthy then I dropped into sweet dark oblivion.

It was the next day before I was finally woken up. The sleep had been good for me and the talk I'd had with Noah had been even better. I felt a lot more relaxed than I had in a long time.

Noah woke me by knocking on the door. I struggled out of sleep and found that someone had put a blanket over me during the night. I felt quietly touched.

"Is the Ambassador here yet?" I asked him.

"Yeah, she got back late last night but she was tired so we felt that it was better to wait until morning. She's had a rest and is having breakfast. Coming?"

I hopped up and slipped back into my shoes, pushing the blanket aside. Then I followed Noah down the length of the train to the dining carriage.

There was no one else up. There wasn't much to do if you didn't actually have an assigned job for that day. So many people just stayed in bed until they got hungry.

Rayna was sitting at a table, eating some soup and looking happy. There were bags under her eyes which suggested that she hadn't got as much sleep as I had, but she was eating with a passion and seemed ready to set off again at a moment's notice. She smiled when she saw me.

"Hello," she said, her eyes sparkling. "Sleep well?"

I nodded and sat down across from her. Noah slid me a bowl, then disappeared deeper into the train on some errand. I dug in and was surprised to find that it was actually beef stew. And it was hot. I thought we'd run out of that ages ago.

"So how did it go last night?" I asked Rayna while tucking in. She grinned.

"Pretty well. I've got maybe another forty people to join us and they should be at the meeting point tomorrow along with everyone else. And Noah has given his word that you guys will be there. He even wrote it down for Cody. It's all going according to plan."

"Good," I said. "So now all we need to do is go and get Cody and bring him and his army here?"

She nodded. "We'll leave right after breakfast. I want to get there early to make sure that he doesn't have the chance to back out of the deal."

We finished eating and were just getting ready to go when something occurred to me. I looked around, puzzled. "Where's Lizzie?" I asked. "I want to say goodbye to her before we go."

Rayna looked at me. "I thought she was with you."

"She was, but she ran off to play while I talked to Noah. I haven't seen her since."

Rayna snorted. For a moment I thought she was going to suggest leaving without finding Lizzie, but then she shook her head and paced off. "Come on," she said. "Let's go ask Noah."

Noah hadn't seen her either and a frantic search started. We combed all the compartments and woke a lot of annoyed kids but there was no sign of the kid we were wanting.

"We can't wait any longer, Jesse," Rayna said at least. "We've got to go."

"We'll keep looking while you're away," Noah assured me. "You'll see her tomorrow."

I nodded to him. "Thanks," I said, then I followed Rayna as she set off. But with every step my heart grew heavier.

We'd lost Lizzie.

CHAPTER 15

Rayna and I walked at the head of the army with Cody, Percy grumbling behind us. I don't think he liked us. Then again, I don't think he liked anyone.

I could see why Rayna had picked Cody to lead the army. Everything was thought out in meticulous detail. The main bunch walked along the road together, not quite in step but at least ordered. About twenty others were constantly darting away from the main body and down side streets, scouting ahead and behind and to the sides to see if there were any chickens about. The one time that there was one nearby we got about ten minutes' notice and managed to hide in the abandoned Sainsbury's, where Cody instructed everyone to take a bit of a break and rest. Then, once it was well gone, we started walking again. And we gained more people every so often as groups that Noah had placed in what he called 'outposts' came trickling in to join him. I was very happy that he was on our side. I would have hated to be against him.

As we passed near Union Street I looked up, a bit

worried that the Brotherhood of the Egg would notice us and tell the chickens. I was hoping that once the chickens were defeated they'd see the error of their ways, but they were still a threat in the meantime. It was pretty hard to hide over one hundred kids walking down a dual carriageway. It seemed that we were lucky, though, as I couldn't see a single flash of white. Thinking about them just made me think of Lizzie and I started worrying again.

Eventually, by a pretty roundabout route, we arrived at the Aberdeen Market, going in the side entrance on Market Street. It was a big place and mostly underground, which made it perfectly suited to our needs. Shops sprawled in several directions, usually places that looked slightly shady or tacky. Or both. The only place there that was of any interest was one of those odd shops that seem to try and sell everything. It had a few useful tools that the Train Station Gang had lifted, but apart from that we'd left it well alone.

Something occurred to me, though. Something that Glen had said about these being real chickens that we faced. If that was true then there might be something in there that I could use against them. But it was only a hunch.

I went into the weird shop and found what I was looking for. I quickly pocketed it and came out again just as Noah's group arrived.

Cody's army had already taken up most of the upstairs of the market, his people sprawled everywhere. At a glance I could see that they'd taken up some pretty good defensive positions as well, places where they could watch the door and have a good angle of attack if needed. Noah was the first through the door and from the look on his face he could see what Cody had done as well. I thought for a second that he was going to turn back and take everyone with him, but he squared his shoulders and walked calmly into the building. I was impressed. Cody's army outnumbered our guys by about ten to three.

Cody had obviously been watching as well because he appeared a moment later, walking towards the doors. "You must be Noah," he said, holding out his hand. Noah glanced at it then shook it abruptly. "Nice to meet you."

"Likewise," Noah replied, then turned and made sure that there was no one left outside. The Train Station Gang hung around for a moment. They bunched together in a group and looked warily at Cody's army. I saw Sam clench his hands into fists. Noah returned and locked gazes with Cody. Tension hung thick in the air. It wouldn't take much for it to snap and calamity to strike.

Rayna saw it too. With a smile she hurried towards them. "Noah, there you are. Did you get here all right?"

He nodded, then turned away from Cody. I saw everyone relax a bit and I let out a breath I hadn't even known I was holding. "Yeah, it wasn't too much trouble. We came as quickly as we could. So when are we doing this?"

"Yes, I'd like to know that as well, Ambassador. Or are we just going to hang out all day?" Cody drawled.

Rayna gave Cody a look. If glares were lasers she could have taken on the chickens by herself with that stare.

"We're waiting for other groups to join us then we're moving out at night. Until then yes, we're just 'hanging out.' So find somewhere to sit and just relax."

Cody's army settled back into their seats and the Train Station Gang, at a nod from Noah, spread out as well. Soon they'd settled down and a murmur of conversation filled the building. But it wasn't quite as relaxed as Rayna had hoped. The two groups kept to themselves and eyed each other suspiciously.

Throughout the course of the day more groups trickled in, usually between five and fifteen people. I was surprised that there were that many groups still around in Aberdeen. The fact that Rayna had been able to reach them all and convince them to join her was more surprising still. These smaller bands would sometimes mingle with one or other of the groups already there, but this did little to lighten the atmosphere.

"Worried?" I asked Rayna at one point. She looked at me and raised an eyebrow.

"What do you mean?" she asked.

"Well they don't seem to be getting along that well."

She sniffed haughtily and stalked away. "They don't have to like each other, they just have to do this," she called over her shoulder.

Eventually night began to fall. I watched as the light behind the glass doors to the outside slowly grew grey and then dwindled to black. Finally, Rayna began to call people together. Everyone crowded around where they could and I was uncomfortably aware that they had separated into three groups. Those who were with Cody seemed to be on the left while those with Noah took the right. The rest hung around uncomfortably in the middle.

"You all know what we're here to do," Rayna shouted out over the hubbub, quieting the crowd. "Here's the plan. We'll leave here tonight and make our way towards where the chickens' signal tower is. Before it gets light we'll hide in houses near them. Then some of us will sneak round the back with sledgehammers and other tools. The rest of you will attack from the front. The front group are to cause as much chaos as possible, attracting the attention of the chickens. While they're distracted, the second group will destroy their power source, rendering them defenceless.

"This could be the end of the control that the chickens have over us, the fear they make us live in. Finally we will be able to walk the streets out in the open. You know the plan. We can do this!"

There was a faint ragged cheer but it died after a second.

"Can I just say that I really hate this plan?" Cody said loudly.

Rayna crossed her arms and stared him down. "Noted. But what else are we supposed to do?"

Cody got up from the chair that he'd been sitting in. Instantly all of his followers did as well, gathering behind him. Noah frowned and then he and the Train Station Gang went to stand behind the Ambassador. Some of the other groups followed him but most kept to the side, watching the development warily. Cody was smiling widely, as if this was all going the way he wanted.

"I'm not saying that taking the chickens down isn't important, I'm just saying that the plan is dumb. We should take time to think about this."

"You've had three days to think of something better." Rayna advanced on him, her eyes blazing. "This is all we can do. There's nothing else. So this is what we do. Tonight. We take the chickens down."

"Stop, misbelievers!"

The voice rang out from behind me and I turned to see Egbert standing there, the Brotherhood of the Egg clustered around him. They must have got in from the Union Street entrance, which wouldn't have been guarded. Cody must have believed no other kids would risk being on Union Street. He'd been wrong.

Egbert paced forward, a huge grin on his face, his cult streaming along in his wake. Against our dirty clothes their robes seemed to shine even whiter, despite the ugly mess of feathers. "We are the Brotherhood of the Egg. A little bird told us that you were plotting against our lawful masters and we have come here to stop you."

My stomach froze into a solid block of ice and I quickly scanned the group. There, hiding near the back, was Lizzie. She was still dressed in the clothes we'd given her and she was looking uncertain.

Both Cody and Noah turned away, the tension rising between them in the face of this new threat. "What's this?" Noah asked me.

I stepped forward. "Let me handle this," I told them. They glanced at each other again then nodded in unison.

"Noble Brotherhood," I called, stepping forward and spreading my arms. "What is the matter?"

"You seek to act against our masters in fowl play, Stranger. We cannot allow that. "

"What are they talking about? Who are they?" I heard Noah mutter to Rayna.

"They're a group that worship the chickens and seem to communicate in puns. Jesse can get along with them pretty well."

I heard the sound of him burying his face in his hands. "Of course he can."

I ignored him and focused on trying to convince the Brotherhood.

"But why? If they are as mighty as you say, what does it matter if we ruffle their feathers?"

Egbert took another step towards me, trying to stand on tiptoe so that he could look me in my eye. I crossed my arms and smirked, glad to finally have the height advantage.

"It's an insult. It will not stand. You said you were on the side of the birds. Were you lying?"

"I said that the chickens were the masters because they were the mightiest around. If we can defeat them or even threaten them then why should I worship them?"

The Brotherhood were so surprised at that line of reasoning that they almost forgot to flap and say 'The chickens are our masters!' I pressed on before Egbert could think of a comeback.

"A true master shelters his people and would never do them harm. Could the same really be said for our chicken masters?"

"They do look after us and give us corn. More so than others, who have abandoned us. Like the adults." Egbert practically spat the last part and I felt suddenly sorry for them. On some level we were all missing our parents and during the first few months no one had coped well with their sudden disappearance. I could almost see the way that Egbert and his followers had turned to the chickens for support. Almost. But that didn't make what they were doing right.

"We all miss our parents. But are the birds any better?"

Egbert stamped his foot and faced me squarely. "Yes."

"Don't you see?" Noah yelled at him. "The chickens don't care for you. They'll betray you."

The group looked at him blankly. I thought about it for a moment then translated.

"He says that they'll peck you in the back."

The Brotherhood were looking at each other and muttering. Egbert could see it and tried to get them back on his side.

"Don't be fooled, followers. The chickens are there for us. They will take us under their wing."

I knew I was getting through to them because only about half of them did the stupid mutter and flap thing. The rest just looked at him blankly.

"Why should we listen to you?" I demanded, abruptly switching tack. "You don't even know what to call them."

"What?"

"They aren't chickens. They're either hens or roosters. If you don't even know what they're properly called then why should we believe anything that you have to say?" Everyone looked confused when I said that.

Time to finish up.

"Look, how about this?" I stepped forward, past Egbert, towards the crowd, holding my hands wide. "I want to believe in the chickens as well. Think of this as a test of faith. If we act against the birds and nothing happens then we'll know we were wrong and we'll accept the rightful consequences. If not, if we really do harm them, then there's no reason to follow them, is there?"

This caused more muttering. I stepped back. I didn't like having Egbert behind me. I looked at them in satisfaction. I probably wasn't going to be able to change their minds, but hopefully I'd said enough to make them go away and not interfere.

"It doesn't matter," Egbert said. "It is already too late for you."

Oh man. That really didn't sound good. "What do you mean?" I asked him.

He grinned at me. "We already contacted our masters before we came here. They are on their way."

I looked at him blankly for a moment then turned to our assembled army.

"Everyone run!" I screamed. "THE CHICKENS ARE COMING!"

They ran, pushing past one another in desperation to get to the exit. The first few shimmied their way passed the wedged boards and ran out into the street, scattering in all directions. I don't know where they were going, but they were fast.

Just not fast enough.

I heard a few screams, abruptly cut off and ending in metallic clacking sounds. Suddenly the flow of people reversed. "They're outside already!" someone yelled.

Then the Brotherhood of the Egg began to act. Even with the doubts I might have managed to sow in a few of their minds they weren't going to ignore any orders that they had been given in front of their masters. They all joined hands and started shoving, pushing everyone back towards the doors where the chickens were waiting. They began clucking as they did so, while Egbert stood at their head and crowed.

The Brotherhood were outnumbered but they were working together, almost as if they'd practised. They managed to cut us off and box us in, forcing us back one step at a time. The first few people were shoved out through the doors and I heard a few more sounds of gigantic chickens plucking up their prey.

We would have been doomed if it wasn't for Egbert's ego. After a moment he snapped out a command and the Brotherhood stopped. We strained against them but they held fast. Egbert, meanwhile, was making his way through the crowd in the direction of the door. He went outside.

"Oh great masters, see this offering we give to you." I turned, fighting against the crowd, and jumped up on a nearby table to get a good view of what was happening. I could see Egbert standing there, his robes glowing in the sunlight. He was standing outside and before him were the two gleaming legs of a giant chicken. "Take these rebels and let us...."

I bet he had some big grand speech worked out, but I never got to hear the end of it. With one abrupt movement the chicken bent down and examined him. Egbert faltered, staring into one of its large, gleaming eyes. It stared back for a moment then raised its head again. I think I saw Egbert give a sigh of relief before it pecked down and snapped him up.

There was silence for a moment, everyone still, no one quite able to understand what had happened. It was like standing on a wall and suddenly losing your balance. I could feel the mood toppling backwards and forwards, with no idea of which way it would fall.

So I decided to give it a push.

"Your leader has been taken by the chickens," I yelled at the Brotherhood. "They don't have any use for you now. They're taking you too."

That was enough. They let go of each other's hands and turned to run towards the other exit at Market Street; the one we'd come in at. Everyone piled after them and I joined at the end.

But it was no good. Before I'd got halfway across the floor everyone was back again, milling around in confusion. "They're out there as well!" someone yelled.

We were trapped.

CHAPTER 16

"All the exits are guarded. There's only one Catcher on the Union Street entrance, but the doorway is narrow and if we tried leaving there it would do the job until more turned up." Noah slammed his fist down in frustration. "There's no way out."

Noah had gone to check it out and was back to where we'd set up a small War Council to try and work out what to do next. There was Rayna, Cody, Noah, Percy and myself. There was also the Brotherhood of the Egg. Since their leader had been eaten they'd attached themselves to me, no matter how hard we tried to shoo them away. I was actually kind of glad they were there. I had been worried that someone would start a fight with them and then people would get hurt. At least here we could keep an eye on them.

"So what do we do now?" I asked. Noah shot a look at Cody.

"Any ideas?" He asked him. "You seem pretty good with tactics."

Cody nodded to Noah to accept the compliment,

though he didn't smirk like he would have an hour ago. "If we can't get out then we've got to stay here. The chickens can't get in without tearing down half the building and they don't want to do that. The Brotherhood isn't forcing us out any more so I don't see that we have to move."

"So we just stay here and wait it out?" Rayna said. Cody turned his cool stare onto her.

"Maybe. Eventually, though, we'll run out of food and then we'll have to go anyway."

"How do we know that they won't go first? They've got the same problem as us, surely?"

Cody shook his head and so did a few others. Even I could see the problem.

"They just need to swap out the guards occasionally. If they send some back to base for food or whatever and take it in turns they can keep us here for as long as they like. They might even have food inside those robots. They might not even need food. What do we know?"

I thought about it for a second and then turned to the Brotherhood. "Do you know anything about the chickens? About how they operate?"

They looked at me with shattered faces and one or two shook their heads. I shrugged. It had been worth a try. But the betrayal by the chickens had obviously hit them hard and they were struggling to recover.

"Why ask them?" Rayna said bitterly. "They're worthless."

"They might have known," I replied. "They were obviously pretty tight with the chickens. I mean they could contact them and everything. What I want to know is why they got attacked now."

"Simple," Cody said from the other side of the table. "The chickens were using them. They must have known that there were lots of kids hiding in the ruins and that at some point those kids might want to fight back against them. So the chickens had the cult watching out for any such activity and reporting it. I guess they'd just outlived their usefulness."

"Forget about them. Let's get back to the problem at hand. What else can we do?"

Cody shrugged. "If we are desperate I guess we could all run at once. The same as with your plan for taking down that stupid signal of yours. We all pile out at once and hope that they can't take us all."

"That's a fairly dumb plan," I said, but softly. No one bothered replying. We all knew it was dumb. We also knew that it was all we could do.

"So do we pick a place for us all to meet up or what?" Noah asked. "Or do we just run and hope to all meet up at some point in the future?"

"Well, could we still go through with the plan? If enough of us get away we might still be able to go after that signal." Rayna watched the others carefully, single-minded as ever. But there was a lot of head shaking.

"We don't even know if we'll be able to get out," Noah pointed out. "And even if we did I don't think that there's going to be enough of us. I hate to say it but the chickens have beaten us. They've won."

"No." Rayna slammed her fist down onto the table, shaking it slightly. "We can't let them win. As long as we're still fighting they won't have won."

There was silence for a moment then Cody leaned towards her. "Ambassador. We've lost. We might be able to do something at some point in the future but right now we need to acknowledge that they've won. All right?"

Her eyes flashed and it looked like she was going to argue some more. I reached out and gripped her shoulder, just like she had done before for me. She looked at me and I could see the sadness in her eyes. "All right," she whispered. "For now."

There was a sigh of relief from around the table. "So are we doing this run and scatter thing?" Noah asked. One by one everyone nodded, even Percy. I hadn't even been sure he was listening.

"Well are we all meeting up at one place then? Or are we just...?"

"Chickens!" someone screamed off to the right. I turned to face it, confused. There couldn't be chickens here. They were all outside.

I was wrong. It was the Commandos. And even though they were just the size of an actual chicken, they were still terrifying.

It was first time anyone had ever seen the Commandos in action. They didn't seem laughable any more. I could see their eyes flashing. Some of them were beating the air with their metal wings, actually taking off once or twice. I saw a girl run past screaming with a chicken clinging to her back. It pecked at her and she stopped screaming, falling onto the floor with a confused look on her face till she finally lay full length and unconscious. Then I realised. The chickens must have some sort of sedative on their beaks. They'd put us all to sleep, then drag us out.

Cody and Noah were yelling things, but it was everyone for themselves. Some ran to the doors and got pecked up by the Catchers waiting outside. Others tried fighting the smaller chickens, kicking them away or picking them up and throwing them, but the chickens seemed to be communicating with each other and anyone that who resistance was abruptly mobbed. I could see a few roosters that were squawking loudly and seemed to be directing the others.

I grabbed Rayna and pulled her away from the table and the others. She struggled at first then looked around and nodded, finally accepting that there was no hope left.

We walked carefully through the chaos, trying not to draw any attention. We had to get through the Brotherhood of the Egg. One or two of them yelled and fought the others to get away, but most just stood, unable to accept what they were seeing. In the middle of them I could see Lizzie, tears running down her face. I felt something tug in my heart and immediately veered to the side, grabbing her hand and dragging her with us. I could feel Rayna clutch my hand tightly and turned to see her glaring at me. I know that she didn't like it but something in my face made her decide not to argue. But I knew that if we ever got out of here, somehow, she would have a few choice things to say to me.

I was trying to make it to the Union Street entrance. If it was the mostly lightly guarded then we'd probably be able to get out there. But more chickens were amassing and I got the feeling that we were going to be noticed soon.

I heard a triumphant crow and turned around to see that most of the kids were down. Only a few groups were left. Kids who had listened to Cody and Noah had formed a circle around them, standing on the table and bashing away at any chicken that flew at them. I saw Percy swing a baseball bat and hit a chicken that was aiming for his head. There was a clear chiming noise and it flew straight through the air, hitting the far wall and bouncing off it. The others lashed out with spades and some of the hammers that Rayna had brought. The Brotherhood of the Egg were running around yelling and kicking the odd chicken. They seemed to be trying to make as much noise as they could.

One of the groups that Rayna had sought out was backed into a corner and fighting as best as they could. For a second I thought they might stand a chance. But then a swarm of chickens mobbed them. First one fell, then another, and after a few moments they were all down. The Brotherhood went down next, the chickens finally tranquilising them. As the last member of the Brotherhood went down he turned to look at me and winked. Had all that running and yelling been their way of trying to cover my escape?

It didn't matter. The group on the table couldn't last much longer. They were badly outnumbered. They didn't stand a chance. A chicken fluttered over their heads and landed on Noah, peaking down hard at his scalp. He yelled and then Sam had to catch him as he fell. Cody and Percy fought back to back as more chickens poured in. Then another wave of chickens crashed in and I lost sight of them behind the metal feathers and beaks.

That's when one of the roosters noticed us.

We ran. It was all we could do.

We tore up the stairs and down one of the corridors that I hoped led to the exit. I hadn't been here much and it was like a small underground maze. Though if I was lucky then the chickens wouldn't know which way we'd gone and would have to split up. This way me, Lizzie and Rayna might get away.

I saw signs for the exit up ahead, as well as the odd feather that must have fallen from the Brotherhood's robes. We sprinted for the exit. Behind us we could hear the odd squawking and the click of metal claws as the chickens hurried after us.

Our luck ran out a moment later. When Noah had

got back from checking out this exit he must have decided to make sure it was secure. The door was closed and a small barricade had been built across it, made of chairs, tables and a pile of metal buckets.

"Get that down!" I screamed at my companions and grabbed a chair, pulling it away from the greater mass with a giant crash. They joined in, but I knew it was too late. That clacking had caught up with us and I turned to see the chickens advancing. The sight of about ten metal chickens walking towards you is oddly hypnotic. I lost precious time gazing at them in fear before I remembered my plan and shook myself out of it.

"Get behind me and keep working on that barricade!" I yelled. I stepped between the girls and the chickens and shoved my hands into my pockets, hoping against hope that both Glen and my hunch were right.

It was odd, watching the metal chickens walk. They seemed to strut, as if proud of their accomplishments, taking the odd little hop here and there. One chicken would spread his wings and then the others would copy it. It was almost as if I were watching some odd form of dance. A dance that spelled disaster for me.

I waited for them to get closer while behind me furniture fell and buckets rattled. As if sensing that their prey was getting away the chickens suddenly rushed at us, wings spread and squawking.

That was when I acted. At the last possible moment, I whipped the bags of bird seed out of my pockets and swept them at the chickens, spraying the corn everywhere.

Well, Glen was right. No matter what else they were, they were still chickens, and I have never seen a single chicken that didn't immediately try and eat any corn that was put in front of it. I knew that it wouldn't distract them for long. In a second they'd come to their senses and go for us again, but in that instant that we had I grabbed the nearest bucket and slammed it down on the lead rooster. Rayna and Lizzie grabbed buckets as well.

Clang, clang, clang, clang, clang. In seconds all the chickens were trapped underneath the heavy metal buckets. The chickens went mad. They began fluttering back, desperately banging against the sides of the buckets. The buckets began rocking backwards and forwards and we quickly began tearing the rest of the barricade down. It looked like the chickens were going to escape at any time.

We managed to race out of the door just in time, closing and locking it behind us. I breathed a sigh of relief and looked around. We were in a stairwell painted a grubby white with posters plastered over all the walls. We climbed the stairs slowly, careful not to make a sound, then crept down the long corridor that led to the outside. I paused at the mouth of the tunnel and looked around cautiously. The giant chicken that Noah had said was there was nowhere to be seen. It must have moved round to the other entrance when the attack by the smaller chickens began. Whatever the reason, we were safe.

I grabbed the girls' hands and together we fled up the street. I looked around frantically for a place to hide until Lizzie tugged on my hand and led us to the side and through a wrought iron gate. I looked up and saw the Kirk of St Nicholas before me. For a second I thought that she was betraying us again, but then I remembered that the Brotherhood were all gone and probably captured. It would probably be the safest place for us.

Rayna looked dazed and exhausted so I gently pulled her along and up the church steps. She tried moving away at the last instant but I manoeuvred her inside and then closed the doors behind us. A soft boom echoed throughout the church as the doors shut and I let out a sigh of relief. We were safe. For now.

CHAPTER 17

For a while we just sat in a chamber off the main hall and didn't say anything. Lizzie seemed especially cowed. Rayna wouldn't even look at her and eventually she dozed off. I felt like joining her. But I wanted to keep an eye on Rayna.

I don't know how much time went by but eventually she got to her feet. I got up as well. "What are you doing?" I asked her.

She didn't look at me, just stared at the table and started putting her backpack on. "I'm going to take down that signal," she said to me, turning to go.

I darted forward and grabbed her arm. "Rayna, you can't. It's crazy. We needed an army before. What makes you think it's going to be any different now? If anything there's going to be even more chickens there now that they know what we're up to. There's nothing you can do."

"It doesn't matter," she said quietly. "I've still got to do it."

"But there's no way you'll succeed. Not on your own.

We should just get back to surviving."

"That's what you want, isn't it?" Her voice was soft and almost emotionless. "To go back to it all. You don't really care that they got taken. You weren't that close. You have no reason to fight."

Her words hurt me but I tried not to let it show. "Yes, that's what we should do now. It's the sensible thing. I'm going to take Lizzie and try that. Just... surviving. And I want you to come with me."

"I've still got to try."

I tried to think of something else I could say.

"Look, you're the Ambassador. You have knowledge that's too important to be lost. You know where everyone is and you get along with them. They trust you. And you are one of only a few people who know about the signal. Everyone else was taken. You can't just give up!"

"Yes, they were taken! And it was all my fault!" She finally looked up at me and her eyes were swimming with tears. "I was the one who pushed for this. Everyone else tried to warn me, but did I listen? No! I was so obsessed with taking on the chickens that I pressured everyone into it. And I do mean everyone. You think my knowledge is important? You think that I know all the groups around? Well I did. And I contacted them all! Everyone I could lay my hands on, everyone I could contact, every debt that I could call in. I did it all. And they came. There's no one left, except for Glen at the university and whoever he's got with him. Him, you, me, that girl," she pointed at Lizzie, who was looking up at her, startled awake by the shouting. "We're all that's left. And it's all my fault."

She collapsed back into her seat and began sobbing, not even trying to keep her tears back. I stared at her, not sure what to say, the news numbing me inside. No one left? I knew the chickens had got a lot of people but was there seriously nobody left?

Finally Rayna got herself under control and stood back up, tears still streaming down her face. "And that's why I've got to do it," she told me, her voice still trembling slightly from sobs. "Because there's nothing left."

"You could stay here, with me and Lizzie." I felt the words come out, though I wasn't sure why I was saying them. The news had stripped everything out of me. "We need to stick together. Please don't leave."

She cast a scornful glance at the little girl. "I don't think I could," she said. "Not with her. Not with a traitor."

Lizzie jumped to her feet and ran across the stone floor, her shoes slapping pathetically. She lunged forward and fastened herself around Rayna's leg.

"No, please, don't. I'm sorry. I didn't mean it," she cried. Rayna tried to shake her off, but she only gripped tighter. "I'll do anything. I'll give you anything. I'll even show you the eggs! Just please don't leave."

Rayna tried to shake her off again, but what Lizzie

had said connected with something inside me and I felt a sudden warmth flood though me. It was hope.

I walked over to the two struggling girls and knelt down beside them. I gently prised Lizzie's arms from around Rayna's leg. She sobbed again and flung herself at me, wrapping me in a tight hug. I whispered to her, "Lizzie. What eggs?"

Rayna had turned to leave but I called her back. "Rayna, wait. You might want to hear this."

She turned to me with a sneer. "I don't want anything that traitor is offering."

"Just wait. It can't hurt to listen."

She made a noise of disgust but didn't move. I began comforting Lizzie, trying to get her to speak.

"Come on, Lizzie. Answer me. What are these eggs?"

"They're presents from the masters... from the chickens," she sniffled. "We keep them inside the vaults. They're why we're called the Brotherhood of the Egg."

"Can you show them to us? This might be important."

"All right." She carefully let go of me and backed away, her face red from crying.

"Go on, Lizzie. Lead the way."

She led us along a corridor and back outside. Rayna exchanged glances with me, still worried that it might be a trap, but all Lizzie did was lead us around the side of the buildings and down some stone steps to a door. Taking a key from the inside of a nearby bin, she unlocked the door and we stepped inside.

There were several large rooms, like caves hewn in the earth. I had no idea what they had been used for before, but now they held the Brotherhood's most sacred artefacts. The gifts given to them by the chickens.

Eggs. One big one and lots of smaller ones. Metal eggs, laid by metal chickens.

"Hey, Rayna," I said, gazing at them in disbelief.

"What?" she asked, in exactly the same tone of voice I was using. I could tell that she couldn't believe it either.

"Stop me if you've heard this one before. What happens when a hen eats gunpowder?"

Rayna turned to look at me and a fierce grin spread across her face. "I don't know," she said. "What happens when a hen eats gunpowder?"

The moon chose that moment to come out from behind the cloud cover, reflecting light off the metal shells and across my face. I grinned back at Rayna.

"She lays hand gren-eggs."

CHAPTER 18

We quickly made a plan back in the church, sitting round the same table. The atmosphere hummed with hope. We had a chance. It was still a pretty distant one, but it was a chance.

"I wonder how the Brotherhood got all those eggs?" Rayna asked, unable to keep a smile from her face. "I find it hard to believe they were from the chickens."

"They gave us the small ones and taught us how to use them," Lizzie replied, her eyes dancing. "There's a button you press on them and then you throw. But Egbert wanted more. We could only find one of the big ones, though."

"I guess it doesn't matter where they got them as long as we can use them," Rayna continued, ignoring Lizzie completely. "With that big one we can blow up the aerial and get rid of the signal for good."

I frowned, slightly worried. "Do you even know how to activate the big grenade?"

Rayna shook her head. "No, but I bet all I've got to

do is throw one of the smaller ones at it. If the small one blows up then the bigger one will blow up as well. And it'll take the aerial with it."

Then her smile faded. "But we've still got the problem of the chickens. If the signal really is as important to them as we think it is they'll still be guarding it, even if they think that the threat is gone. We'll need some sort of distraction to get them away from there. We can't just overwhelm them with force of numbers any more."

"We could attack them," cried Lizzie, almost overcome with excitement. I shushed her quickly.

"Quiet, Lizzie. There could be some chickens around. We don't want to get caught."

That shut her up. It was obvious that now she truly believed that the chickens were dangerous.

"But we could," she hissed at me. "We could attack them with the eggs."

I smiled at her. "I don't think so. These things managed to fight off the army and tanks. I don't think a few exploding eggs would be able to stop them."

"We need a diversion," Rayna said again. I looked up at her.

"Any idea what would be a good distraction?" I was thinking it over in my head and I felt that cold feeling slither down my neck. I sure could think of something. But it wasn't a good idea.

Rayna was shaking her head. "I guess if we made enough noise somewhere then they'd be forced to come and investigate. But this time it's going to be different. This time we're going to properly think it through. We're not just going to run in."

I sighed and shook my head. "Much as I hate to say this, I think we should act now. I've got an idea that might work and would certainly get you your distraction. But it only works tonight."

She looked at me curiously. "What is it?" she asked. I told her.

"You're crazy," she told me matter-of-factly. "That's insane. It'll never work. You'll be found and caught."

I smiled at her, as if I were afraid of nothing. I was getting good at lying. "That's kind of the point. If I do it right then I should have every chicken in Aberdeen flocking to me. It'll give you enough time to do what you need to."

"No, no, there are only two of us now. If we lose even one then we're done for. We can't split up."

"It's got to happen," I told her, my voice more calm than I was. "I'll take Lizzie and we'll go do it. You take the big egg and go do your thing. Get ready to destroy that signal. We'll meet up after and have a party to celebrate."

She shook her head, lowering it and letting her fringe fall in front of her face. For a second I thought I saw a tear shining between the strands of her hair but when she looked up it was nowhere to be seen. "You're an idiot," she told me seriously. "Are you sure you want to do this?"

I nodded, though I was anything but sure. "We've got a lot to do tonight. So let's get moving."

She shook her head. "You're a moron, Jesse. But a brave one."

I shrugged. "I guess I was just born stupid."

"Do you understand what we're doing?" I asked Lizzie as we walked together down the road. She nodded, though her eyes were wide. I made sure that she was walking a good distance away from the shopping trolley I was pushing. I'd been careful to cushion the eggs in clothes to stop them knocking against one another, but every time it went over a pothole or a crack in the pavement my heart would jump up into my throat. We were walking down King Street again and the moon was alternately shining through the cloud or covering us in darkness. I couldn't help but think about creeping towards Beechgrove a few nights ago and how scared I had been. I wasn't scared now. There was no point. The worst that could happen was that the chickens got me. I just had to make sure that I didn't walk into a car or something and blow Lizzie and me to smithereens.

"I think so," Lizzie replied. "We go and use all these eggs. Then Rayna blows up something so the chickens all stop working?"

"Yeah, basically. We have to draw the chickens away from the signal so that Rayna can use the big egg to stop them receiving commands. That means that we have to get all the chickens to come to us. Then we win, I guess. And we can meet up with her again."

We were just drawing level to the hardware shop I'd seen before. I told Lizzie to watch the trolley and went inside to pick up a few things. I took them out then piled them beside the trolley, staring at them and wondering how I was ever going to get them in. Eventually I took all the eggs out carefully, then put the tools in. I put several layers of clothes on top of them to make sure that they were properly padded and finally put the eggs in on top. Then I put some more clothes around them.

"I really am sorry about what I did before," Lizzie said beside me when we started walking again. I looked at her and smiled. So that was why she'd been so quiet.

"I'm sure you are, but words aren't what makes people know you're sorry."

"Then what is?"

"You show them." I handed her the file and crowbar that I'd taken from inside and put the bolt cutters in my jacket. "Are you OK with those?"

She weighed them in her hands. They were obviously heavy but she held them with determination and nodded. "Yes, Jesse."

"Good. Then let's get walking."

As we set off again she asked, "Why do you need all those shovels and things anyway?"

"You'll see."

We walked for another hour, creeping steadily towards our goal. The walls of Pittodrie were soon visible before us, half hidden by a grassy embankment. It was a very red building, made of red brick and painted red metal, the same colour as the football team strip. My dad had taken me here a couple of times to see the team play. They'd usually lose and Dad would drive me home, complaining about how the Dons could be great again if only we got a decent manager. There was no football here now and hadn't been for a while – but here I was. I just hoped that this time it wouldn't be the usual crushing defeat.

We turned off the road into the parking area and rattled round the side. The moon had gone behind a cloud again and I had to steer the trolley carefully, but I guessed darkness was best. Hopefully, that meant that I couldn't be seen either. Unless the chickens had infrared eyesight or something.

I quickly forced myself to stop thinking about that. This was risky enough as it was.

A door in the side of the stadium was unlocked, but this only increased my feelings that everything was about to go badly wrong. I eased the trolley over the threshold and winced as it bumped slightly. Then we headed carefully down the corridor, through the team changing room and into the tunnel that led to the pitch. Ahead was the massive bulk of our goal.

"And this," I whispered to Lizzie, "is how you show you are sorry. Here we go."

CHAPTER 19

I left Lizzie guarding the trolley and sneaked forward, the grass sinking beneath my feet. I'd been expecting it to be long and neglected, but someone seemed to have been taking care of it. It was the uniform length that the football clubs always demanded. The members of the Brotherhood who guarded this place must have been looking after it.

Right in front of me was the goal I was creeping towards. It was pretty tall, about as big as a house, and there were several of them scattered all over the football field. Giant wooden structures with mesh over the front of them, the insides lit by hanging bulbs; the cages where the chickens kept their captives. They even had the giant cylinders that dispensed water. They looked like the sort of things that battery hens were kept in. I guess that chickens have a sense of humour too.

The sound of chanting drew me to the nearest one – that was where the Brotherhood of the Egg had been put. There were more of them than had been at the market. I guess the chickens had been forced to grab the ones that had been on guard duty outside the stadium as well. They were still wearing their odd clothes. They were sitting in circles chanting weird things that I couldn't quite hear and looking rundown. I wasn't sure how I felt seeing them there. On the one hand they were responsible for everyone else getting caught. On the other hand they also hadn't really meant any harm. They'd just been brainwashed or something. I guess they deserved their redemption as much as Lizzie did. After all, it wasn't only six year olds who got a second chance. So I pulled out the bolt cutters and began chopping away at the wire in the front of their cage.

I'd been doing it for about a minute before someone noticed. I was aware of more whispering spreading throughout the cage and then a crowd suddenly gathered around me. I looked up to see them all staring. It was pretty creepy. One of the boys shuffled forward. He was about my age and quite a bit taller, though I couldn't properly see him in the moonlight.

"Is that you, Stranger?"

I nodded and continued cutting. "Yup. Thought you guys might like to be rescued."

"Stranger..." They all said in unison. I felt uncomfortable and began to work more quickly.

"Stop! You cannot do this!" I looked up to see Egbert standing over me. He'd been sitting in a corner of the cage, being ignored by everyone else. He was looking pretty bedraggled and his rooster's comb was sagging.

I guess being betrayed by the chickens hadn't been easy on him.

"Can't do what?" I asked him. He glared at me.

"We are here because our masters wanted us to be. We can't do anything that disobeys them like this. They are just testing us."

"Well, you go on believing that and you stay there. I'm not forcing anyone to come. I'm just opening the way if they choose to."

I finished cutting and a big hole opened up, large enough for a kid to squeeze through. I got to my feet and looked at the one who had talked to me first. "You coming? Or are you staying here?"

He bowed his head. "I am coming, Stranger."

I grinned at him. "Good. You're in charge of everyone who wants to leave. You make sure they do what I tell you." I gave him instructions, then stood aside, letting him out. He quickly scampered away and I slapped him on the back, then went to some of the other cages. I glanced back briefly over my shoulder after I'd taken a few steps. They were all gone. Only Egbert was left standing in the cage. Boy, did he look mad.

After a bit of sneaking around I managed to find the cage where Noah and Cody were being kept, along with everyone else who had held out at that table. They must have been given several doses of the tranquiliser because they were all still unconscious. I just hoped I could wake the leaders. Everything hinged on them being able to control everyone else.

I slowly crept towards the cage and began cutting the mesh again.

"Hey, Noah. Cody!" I hissed. "Wake up."

No one stirred. Once I had cut a hole big enough for my hand I reached in and grabbed Sam's leg. I shook it and he began to wake up. But not quickly enough. Looking nervously around, I took a bottle of water from my backpack and unscrewed the top. Then with a quick jerk I sent all the water straight into his face.

Sam woke with a yell and I quickly shushed him, looking around again. Eventually the chickens would realise what we were doing, but the longer it was before that happened the better. He glared blearily up at me then seemed to realise what was happening. I could vaguely see his jaw drop open, then he wiped the water out of his eyes and he began waking everyone else up. They roused with small groans and faint yelps, but soon they were all staring at me.

"Jesse, what are you doing?" Noah asked me once he'd pushed his way to the front, Cody not far behind him.

"I'm saving you," I told him. "I think I can get you out of here."

He looked at me for a moment then shook his head. "I don't think you can. They've got things on our legs." He held out his to demonstrate and I saw a ring of metal with a blinking red light shining through his socks. "They've got to be tracking us or something."

"According to Rayna, they only activate once you

leave the stadium," I told him. "She heard it from someone who had tried to do this before. As soon as you leave the field they set off the alarms and the chickens come for you. But don't worry. I've got a plan."

"Of course you do," said Cody. "Your last plan was rubbish and is the reason we're here in the first place. Why should we trust you with this one?"

"Feel free not to trust me. Use one of the many other ways to escape," I replied. He scowled for a moment then nodded, acknowledging my point. "But there's a difference between this one and the last. That was Rayna's plan. And this is mine."

"So what is it?" he asked. I told him and got to enjoy the shock that floated across his face.

"You're insane," he told me, but I saw Percy at his shoulder, grinning. At least one person liked the plan.

"Yeah, people say that," I told him. "I just see it as a way to keep life interesting. Now are you in or not?"

After a second he nodded and everyone else joined in. I cut the last link and the mesh fell away. Everyone flooded out and I pointed them in the direction of the trolley. "Get your weapons over there. There's some more bolt cutters as well. I'll need some guys helping me."

They went at it with a will as I started on the next cage. There were about ten in all and I was only halfway done when someone joined me to help. I looked around and saw others at other cages. Everyone would be free in about ten minutes. Good, right on schedule.

While I was just finishing the last cage I felt a tap on my shoulder and turned to see Lizzie standing there. "What is it?" I asked.

"Egbert's gone. I watched him creep out of the cage and through one of the doors over there." She pointed at the edge of the stadium and I could just make out an open door. Then I realised that it was getting a lot darker than it had been and I looked up to see that the clouds over the moon had thickened. It looked like we were in for rain soon. I had no idea if that was good or bad.

"All right. Go find Noah and tell him that the chickens are coming."

She nodded and ran off and I sighed as I turned back to the cage, cutting the last few people free. I'd hoped that Egbert would have changed after the chickens turned on him, that he wouldn't still regard them as his masters. But I guess I'd been wrong. He hadn't changed. And he'd just gone to betray everyone to the chickens again.

If I hadn't been expecting it I might have felt a bit upset.

Noah was pushing his way through the crowd, heading towards one of the cages. Cody was already standing on top of it and Percy gave Noah a boost to help him up. The two leaders stood together and addressed the freed kids.

"We don't have much time, so listen closely. We've got out but the chickens know it and they're coming."

A scared murmur spread through the crowd at his words and people towards the back began trickling away, turning and walking towards the doors. But at Noah's next words they all turned round and came back.

"You might have noticed that you have things attached to your legs. Apparently they're tracking devices. As soon as you step outside the pitch, they turn themselves on and the chickens will be able to find you."

Cody took over talking. "But we have a plan. Jesse here showed up with some files for us to use. We can cut those trackers right off you. The problem is that there aren't enough to go around. So we need to hold out here for a bit. We've got weapons and we should be able to hold off the chickens."

"What if we can't?" some kid in the front row yelled out. Cody fixed him with his merciless smile.

"Then please, by all means, leave. We won't keep anyone here who doesn't want to be. I'm sure you could keep running for at least an hour before the chickens eventually found you."

Noah frowned at Cody. "Of course we might keep them busy enough to let you get away but we can't promise anything. So do whatever you feel safest with."

The kid nodded, looking scared but staying where he was. A couple did disappear, but most stayed. Cody nodded to himself, pleased.

"Right then. Please see the guys in the weird white robes. They'll give you your weapons. It's mostly shovels, but we should be able to beat those small chickens."

"Commandos," I whispered at him. He stared at me a second then shrugged.

"They should be able to beat the Commandos. We'll start removing the trackers right away."

Fifteen minutes later there was still no sign of the chickens. I shifted on my feet uneasily, the crowbar held in my hands. I wanted to run. I really, really wanted to grab Lizzie and get out of there. I mean, I didn't have a tracker. Neither did she. But Cody was keeping a close watch on me and I didn't think I'd be able to make it. And this could be our last chance to stop the chickens. I was needed here and though I wanted to run there was no way I was going to.

When I'd thought up the plan I hadn't thought about the long wait, each second expecting the sound of the clawed feet on the road outside. If they could just get on with it then it would be better. Anything would be better than the waiting.

And then I got my wish.

There was a scream from over by the stands and kids started running away. I squinted through the darkness and saw a tide of the smaller chickens flowing along the seats from a box higher up. There were more of them than I was expecting.

Then Cody stepped forward with Percy beside him,

both holding shovels. He began barking out orders and more kids lined up with him. I walked forward as well and we stood together, watching the smaller chickens get closer and closer.

Then with a yell Percy ran forward, swinging his shovel. He caught a Commando in mid-leap and it was flung backwards into the others. Other kids followed him and soon the air was filled with flying chickens. It was almost like Pittodrie had turned into a baseball field and we were hitting nothing but home runs.

Some of the kids weren't fast enough and got pecked; collapsing unconscious before we could do anything. We were slowly pushed back, losing a couple of kids every few moments. But we were just the ones who had acted first. More and more people came running to help. The line held, then slowly we began pushing the chickens back. The ones we hit got back up again and came charging back towards us, but more warily. We had made them fear us, even if we couldn't do much more then sling them around.

I kept my eye on the sky, waiting for the moment that I knew would come.

Then it happened. A low droning sound filled the sky and one of the giant chickens sailed over the walls of the stadium and landed in front of one of the goal posts.

Things froze for a moment and another landed next to the first. Then another, until there were three Catchers towering over everything surrounding them. Then the smaller chickens rushed us again.

"Aim them towards the big ones," Cody yelled and adjusted his grip on his weapon, sending the next chicken that leapt at him clanging off one of the giant ones. Others followed his lead and several chickens ricocheted off and through the goal posts. There were definitely more goals scored with chickens than Aberdeen usually scored with footballs.

The giant chickens paced forward and the army scattered, kids running in every direction. It was instant chaos. Kids and Commandos were running everywhere. The kids were still swinging their weapons, but more and more of them were falling.

I had to do something.

I ran right at the lead chicken and swung my crowbar, hitting it in the side with a bell-like chime. It stopped walking and looked down at me, tilting its head to one side. I could almost see the confused look on its face, like it couldn't believe anything could be that stupid. I hit it again, then turned and ran off. "Come on!" I yelled at it. "What's the matter? You chicken?"

It obviously decided that I was stupid enough to get taken out because it began stepping after me. I ran a short distance in front of it, then stopped and turned, the goal post outlined behind me. I could feel people's eyes upon me, so I shouted out loud and clear.

"You just made a mistake, feather-face. Because this is the penalty box..."

It reached me and pecked down, screeching as it did so. I held the egg that I'd taken from my pocket and threw it into the chicken's mouth. Then I dodged and rolled to the side.

"... and it doesn't reward fowl play."

The chicken just stood there for a moment, as if it didn't realise what had just happened. Then there was the sound of a hollow boom from inside it and a wisp of smoke curled up from its beak. Its feathers rattled against its side and several flew off. It gave a last squawk and keeled over, hitting the ground with a bang. A hatch at the top sprang open and a chicken, a real chicken, the only one I'd seen apart from the Leader on TV, jumped out. It flapped its wings and disappeared into the night. I stared after it in shock, then I became aware of cheering all around me. The chickens had backed off for a moment to regroup and I looked to see that our army had reformed. I grinned at them.

Then droning filled the sky and giant chicken after giant chicken fell from the sky, landing on the ground and surrounding us. The cheering died away and we all huddled together.

"Looks like they're re-cooping their losses," I muttered to myself and heard someone snigger behind me. I turned slightly and saw it was Percy. He was covered in sweat and seemed to have been in the thick of the fighting, but there was a huge grin plastered across his face and it looked like he was having the time of his life.

"Good one," he said. "Got any more of those grenades?"

"Not on me," I told him. He shrugged.

"We'll find some way to do this. Got a plan?"

"Yup. Just watch."

The chickens began advancing towards us again then there was a cry from behind them. "Let's stuff 'em!"

Then grenades began raining down. I looked past the chickens and saw that they were being thrown with considerable enthusiasm by the Brotherhood of the Egg, who had been hiding in the seats. Explosions started going off and everyone started cheering again. Then the fighting began.

For a while we held our own. But eventually the explosions stopped. Either we'd run out of grenades, or the Commandos had rushed the stands and the Brotherhood kids were now all unconscious. More Catchers had landed in the middle of the fighting. There were about fifteen striding about. And gradually we were whittled down to a last desperate group, our backs against each other, surrounded by a sea of metal.

"Well," Cody muttered beside me. "I guess the Ambassador's plan really wouldn't have worked after all." His voice was shaking. I think it was the first time I'd heard him afraid.

"Yeah, it would have been nice to know there were this many chickens around," Noah answered, clearly terrified. I didn't think they knew they were talking to each other. Either that or they were too tired to care that they hated each other. I knew how they felt. My arms could barely hold my weapon and I was tempted to just drop it and sink to my knees. But I couldn't. I would not let the chickens win.

One last chicken fell from the sky and took a step towards us. I thought it looked like a leader. It had a huge comb that towered over the rest of them and in the flickering light of a few fires that we had started its body looked more gold than the others.

"Looks like they think they rule the roost," I muttered, too tired to think up something better. I closed my eyes. I could hear the chickens coming at us and there were so many of them. I just couldn't bear to see them coming.

But at that second, I heard a distant boom echo over the silent city. My head snapped up and I looked about, almost convinced that it was thunder. But the clouds weren't thick enough for thunder.

"Sorry guys," I said to the approaching birds. "But I think your signal just got scrambled." Then with a yell I lifted my crowbar one last time and charged forward.

I aimed right at the golden one, waving my crowbar about and screaming at the top of my lungs. At first it stared at me in astonishment. But then I could almost see the intelligence go out of its eyes. It didn't matter that it was more than twice my size and weighed even more. It was suddenly just a chicken.

It turned and ran, flapping its wings and hopping in an ungainly manner, and the rest of its flock went with it. They reached the stands and crashed up them, sending chairs flying. Finally, they disappeared over the stadium's rim. I ran a few more steps then flopped over and lay on the ground, unable to get up. I heard some people talking and cheering nearby but I ignored them. I just lay there, staring at the sky and laughing. I was vaguely aware of Lizzie dropping down next to me. I reached out and squeezed her hand.

We had done it. The chickens were gone.

CHAPTER 20

It was a week later and we'd finally got round to having that party.

There wasn't a functioning chicken left in Aberdeen. After the battle we'd dragged or carried everyone who had been hit by the Commandos back inside so they could be warm. We watched over them until they'd come to.

Most people had got through the battle in surprisingly good condition. There were a couple who were pretty groggy from being tranquilised, and everyone had bruises, but that was it. I was worried about the guys pecked up by Catchers, who had then run off with the kids still inside them – but they turned up over the next few days. They said that they'd woken up to find that the Catchers were just lying there, hatches built into their heads open and empty. The chickens that had been inside them were nowhere to be seen.

After that Aberdeen was ours.

It was weird at first, being able to walk around

the city in broad daylight without being afraid of capture. Everyone had kept to their groups for the most part, but some were beginning to spread out, go back to their homes if they could. Rayna had found a few other groups that had managed to hide from everyone and was slowly getting them used to the idea that the chickens had been defeated. They took some convincing.

But the amazing thing about it was that it brought some families back together. Rayna had found her sister Hazel while blowing up the mast; she was one of the few Brotherhood members left at Beechwood. Some other kids had siblings who had been one of Egbert's people, or who had been in other groups in different parts of Aberdeen.

So to celebrate our freedom and bring everyone together we'd thrown a huge party.

The Bon Accord shopping centre was the perfect place for it, on the upper floor where there had once been an eating area. Before, it had been too close to the Brotherhood of the Egg to be safe, but now we could come and go without a care. The sunlight streamed in through the glass roof, illuminating all the tables where kids were mingling, laughing and tucking into food. The grub wasn't much better than we'd had before, but for once we weren't rationing it. There was also a lot of corn. The Brotherhood had showed us where the chickens had kept their supplies and we'd happily looted it.

I walked around, passing between different tables and catching snatches of conversation. I smiled as I passed the Library Gang, who were sitting in a corner, gazing wide-eyed at all the food. In another corner, Billy sat next to Paul, telling anyone who would listen that he'd once taken down a Catcher single-handed. Cody and Noah sat at either ends of the hall, keeping their distance from each other. They seemed to have called a truce after the battle. They still didn't like each other, but I think they had a kind of grudging respect for one other.

Glen was messing about with a projector, screen and TV at one edge of the hall, a group of five-year-olds running and screaming all around him. He'd turned up with them and glared at Rayna, as if daring her to say anything. I guess all that food hadn't just been for him after all. Lizzie was with them, shrieking as loudly as any of them. It was good to see her having fun.

I gave Glen the plate that I'd been carrying and sat beside him as he stopped fiddling with wires and leads. "What are you doing?" I asked.

He swept a big load of corn into his mouth with his fork and chewed for a few moments before swallowing and answering. "The President of the USA is supposed to be making a speech about the chickens soon. I thought it would be worth seeing."

One of the kids with him tripped on something and went sprawling. Glen immediately put down his food and went over to help the boy up and inspect his knee. I watched, feeling slightly uneasy. I couldn't believe that I'd been so wrong about him. He was actually really kind.

"So where did the kids come from?" I asked, once the tears had stopped flowing and Glen was about to eat again. He shrugged.

"Most of them were in a daycare centre right next to my dad's office. A couple of others were just lost. You know what it was like on the day. Chaos. I just rounded up as many as I could and took them with me. I dunno. I've got a nephew down south – those crying kids made me think of him."

"That was pretty good of you."

"It was the right thing to do."

He finished the plate and went back to the TV. I picked it up and wandered back to my table.

On my way I passed the Brotherhood of the Egg, sitting by themselves. A lot of them had split off once the chickens betrayed them, joining other groups or forming new ones of their own. But a solid core of them still remained. They might have been drawn to the chickens, but they'd been sticking together and looking out for one another for the last few months. I guess that sort of bond doesn't go away overnight.

Rayna was with them, weirdly. She wanted to sit next to her sister Hazel. I'd heard some of what had happened the night of the battle. The chickens had been snapping up the Brotherhood up in Beechgrove as well, thinking that they didn't need them any more. Hazel had been on sentry duty at the time and Rayna had managed to convince her to help, but after blowing up the mast they'd been mobbed by Commandos. When they came round, the chickens had gone.

I knew Hazel by sight but I hadn't spoken to her much. I ambled over. One of the Brotherhood saw me coming and smiled.

"Stranger," he said in greeting, and the rest of the table copied him. I guess some habits are hard to kick.

"Hey guys," I said, waving vaguely. I turned to Rayna. "How are things going?"

"Fine," she said through gritted teeth. She didn't look fine. Although they were sitting together she and her sister weren't talking much.

"I'm Jesse," I said, turning to Hazel. She smiled at me, bright and lively, and held out her hand.

"I know who you are. It's nice to meet you."

We shook.

"Nice to meet you too. So what are you planning on doing now?"

Rayna's scowl deepened. I think I just hit a touchy subject.

"I'm staying with my friends here in the Brotherhood," Hazel replied, with a sideways glance at her sister. "We've got a lot to make up for and I'd like to be a part of that."

"Well, that's very..." I began but Rayna stood up and grabbed my arm.

"Come on, Jesse. I promised Noah I'd eat with your gang."

"All right. See you around, Hazel." I waved goodbye as Rayna towed me off, then shook her off and turned to her. "What's up with you?"

She shrugged. "I don't see why she's got to stay with those freaks. She can hang around with me."

"Those 'freaks' are her friends," I pointed out. "I'm guessing this is an argument you've been having all week."

She nodded. "She'll come to her senses sooner or later. Come on, I want more food. Where are you sitting?"

My seat was with the Train Station Gang, crammed in a corner by a sushi restaurant, with Sam on one side. We squeezed Rayna in on the other. Sam was pretty hyper. He'd been reunited with a sister who had been hiding in Hazlehead and seemed to think that I'd been responsible for that happening. He was sitting there now, with one arm around her, eating corn on the cob like there was no tomorrow.

"I misjudged you, Jesse," he said, for the fifth time. "I used to think that you were a little coward who only looked out for yourself. But look at all you've done. The chickens are beaten and it's all because of you. Let me tell you this; you've got guts."

He held out his hand and I shook it gratefully. He was getting better. At least he'd stopped trying to hug me.

"You know this isn't the end, right Sam?" Rayna said from my other side. She was still upset about her sister. "The chickens will be back."

Sam wasn't in any mood to listen. "And we'll beat them again. They don't have the signal any more. They can't get into the city. Without that what can they do?"

I stopped listening to the argument and my mind drifted. There had been no sign of my brother in any of the groups. I felt hopeful, somehow, that he was OK. I had faith in him. I told myself to stop thinking about it, and concentrated on filling my belly with as much food as I could. A movement caught my eye and I looked up to see the crying girl from the sleeper train and her sister, sitting together and holding hands very tightly. I smiled to myself.

The projector flickered into life and a hush spread across the hall. I craned my neck and could see the President of the USA on the screen. He was standing at a podium, surrounded by grave looking men in uniform, a picture of an eagle behind.

"... because now we know more about them. We know their weakness. We know where they came from. They are not the alien invaders that we were led to believe. They are just chickens."

He looked straight at the camera. "We have learned that they are merely a failed experiment. The UK government were developing them to deploy in place of soldiers in our platforms of war. We've all seen their fearsome leader, the chicken in the funny hat. Our

enemy is deserving of no more than our contempt –
and maybe some barbecue sauce."

He paused while the journalists laughed. "They
maintain their intelligence through signal masts. We
will take them all down. They get all their orders from
their leader. He will fall. We and our allies will fall
upon these metal monstrosities and drive them back
to where they came from. We have suffered their
advances for far too long. It's about time we clipped
their wings. And together, we will prevail. Thank you."

He stepped back from the podium and a bunch of
reporters started shouting questions. In the hall, kids
were turning to each other, cheering and laughing.

I couldn't help it. I smiled. It hadn't been easy. The
last few months had left us all a little hard-boiled. But
now everything was looking sunny side up.

We were finally safe.

Fergus can't believe it when his brand-new watch starts going backwards. Then he crashes (literally!) into gadget-loving Murdo and a second mystery comes to light: cats are going missing all over the neighbourhood.

As the two boys start to investigate, they find help in some unexpected places.

 Also available as an eBook

discoverkelpies.co.uk

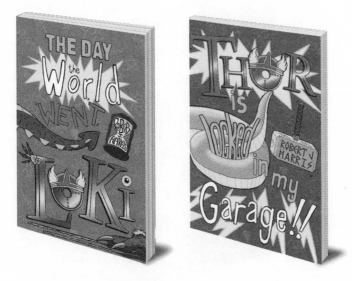

Lewis and Greg *might* have accidentally summoned Loki, the Norse god of mischief. Not to mention his hammer-wielding big brother Thor, trapped in the boys' garage... But it wasn't their fault!

With a gang of valkyries chasing them from St Andrews to Asgard, can the troublesome twosome outwit Loki and save the day?

 Also available as eBooks

discoverkelpies.co.uk

Mischievous fairies? Smelly troll? Werewolf snatching your sheep? Email the Really Weird Removals company!

Luca and Valentina's Uncle Alistair runs a pest control business. But he's not getting rid of rats. The Really Weird Removals Company catches supernatural creatures! When the children join Alistair's team they befriend a lonely ghost, rescue a stranded sea serpent, and trap a cat-eating troll.

Visit **reallyweirdremovals.com** for help with your paranormal pests.

 Also available as an eBook

discoverkelpies.co.uk